S0-ABQ-070

THROWING OUT THE GAUNTLET . . .

Dex grabbed Blake's forearm and hauled down on it, keeping the blow from reaching the helpless Eleanor. Giving the big man no time to react, Dex stepped in and drove his elbow into his solar plexus, emptying the man's lungs and turning Blake pale as the linen wrappings that held his broken jaw in place. Dex took half a step backward and weighed his choices.

Fairness demanded that he pause and give Blake a chance to recover.

But then again, decent and honorable men do not go around beating up women.

No, Dex concluded, Blake was not a man given to decency and honor.

And besides, Dex didn't like him.

So, with deliberate malice, Dex planted his best right-hand smack onto the linen-padded shelf of Blake's broken jaw. Blake's eyes widened, then rolled back in his head, and he passed out cold.

"I think," Dex said, "you'd best have somebody carry him to your town doctor."

DON'T MISS THESE
ALL-ACTION WESTERN SERIES
FROM THE BERKLEY PUBLISHING GROUP

THE GUNSMITH by J. R. Roberts
Clint Adams was a legend among lawmen, outlaws, and ladies. They called him . . . the Gunsmith.

LONGARM by Tabor Evans
The popular long-running series about U.S. Deputy Marshal Long—his life, his loves, his fight for justice.

SLOCUM by Jake Logan
Today's longest-running action Western. John Slocum rides a deadly trail of hot blood and cold steel.

BUSHWHACKERS by B. J. Lanagan
An action-packed series by the creators of Longarm! The rousing adventures of the most brutal gang of cutthroats ever assembled—Quantrill's Raiders.

DIAMONDBACK by Guy Brewer
Dex Yancey is Diamondback, a southern gentleman turned con man when his brother cheats him out of the family fortune. Ladies love him. Gamblers hate him. But nobody pulls one over on Dex . . .

WILDGUN by Jack Hanson
Will Barlow's continuing search for his daughter, kidnapped by the Blackfeet Indians who slaughtered the rest of his family.

DIAMONDBACK

DEAD MAN'S HAND

♦ ♦ ♦

Guy Brewer

J
JOVE BOOKS, NEW YORK

If you purchased this book without a cover, you should be aware that this book is stolen property. It was reported as "unsold and destroyed" to the publisher and neither the author nor the publisher has received any payment for this "stripped book."

This is a work of fiction. Names, characters, places, and incidents are either the product of the author's imagination or are used fictitiously, and any resemblance to actual persons, living or dead, business establishments, events, or locales is entirely coincidental.

DIAMONDBACK: DEAD MAN'S HAND

A Jove Book / published by arrangement with
the author

PRINTING HISTORY
Jove edition / August 2000

All rights reserved.
Copyright © 2000 by Penguin Putnam Inc.
This book may not be reproduced in whole or part,
by mimeograph or any other means, without permission.
For information address: The Berkley Publishing Group,
a division of Penguin Putnam Inc.,
375 Hudson Street, New York, New York 10014.

The Penguin Putnam Inc. World Wide Web site address is
http://www.penguinputnam.com

ISBN: 0-515-12888-0

A JOVE BOOK®
Jove Books are published by The Berkley Publishing Group,
a division of Penguin Putnam Inc.,
375 Hudson Street, New York, New York 10014.
JOVE and the "J" design
are trademarks belonging to Penguin Putnam Inc.

PRINTED IN THE UNITED STATES OF AMERICA

10 9 8 7 6 5 4 3 2 1

◆ 1 ◆

Anything more than a mouthful is wasted. That's how the old saying went, and Dexter Yancey quite thoroughly agreed.

In principle.

But this . . . ah, this was waste on such a magnificent scale that the normal dictates of logic and, yes, even personal preferences simply did not apply.

Yancey stretched, blinked, contemplated with immeasurable joy the sight of Candalaria Gomez—better known in some circles as Candy Cane—as the lady completed her preparations for, well, for whatever was yet to come.

The lady—politeness, to say nothing of outright gratitude, prompted him to use the term with a certain degree of latitude rather than hewing to exact meaning—had just removed her chemise, thus placing on full display a set of breasts that were shaped like ripe watermelons. The primary difference between Candy's breasts and a pair of fully grown melons was that the breasts were the larger.

"Oh my," he whispered, his voice made quiet by the mixture of awe and admiration that filled him.

Candy's answering giggle came out as a high-pitched squeal somewhat akin to the sound a shoat makes when it is picked up and held upside-down. But then what the hell, no one is perfect. Dex closed his ears and concentrated on the extremes laid out before his astonished eyes.

Candy was fully aware of the effect she had on men. It was, after all, her stock in trade. She paused for a moment to give him the benefit of the full, nigh unbelievable sight. Then she completed the much practiced task of disrobing, stepping out of her cotton knickers and kicking them aside. All right, so she wasn't tidy. He hadn't come up here to inspect her housekeeping abilities.

"Wonderful," he said.

"You like what you see, honey?"

"I like what I see, yes."

Candy placed a palm under each boob and lifted, picking them up as if laying them onto a shelf for display. Dex wondered what those knockers weighed. Ten pounds? He'd have bet they did.

A smile flickered across his face as a thought came to him. What would happen, he wondered, if he escorted Candy to a carnival and invited one of those professional guessers of weight to take a crack at these twin mounds.

It would be scandalous, of course. But fun. If there was a carnival anywhere close by . . .

Candy came closer, leaning forward so the tips of her nipples brushed lightly against Dex's shirt. Those nipples were as thick as a thumb if a tiny bit shorter. Big as the last joint on a man's thumb anyhow. And just as hard. Dex had no idea what had Candy so aroused, but the fact bode well for the remainder of the evening.

"Aren't you gonna get undressed, honey?" she invited.

"Now you know something? That's just exactly what I had in mind to do next."

With Candy's expert assistance it took Dex practically no time at all to shed his dark gray swallowtail coat, black riding boots and pale gray breeches. He was glad to see that she was not so casual with her, um, guest's clothing as she was with her own. She folded and arranged his things with reasonable care, then plunked Dex's pearl gray planter's hat on top of the pile. She warily looked at but was careful not to touch the gloves, cane and pair of revolvers he'd already placed onto the dresser. By the time Candy was done with her arranging, Dex was as naked as she.

"Very nice," she said as she very frankly looked him up and down. She she even sounded as if she indeed meant it.

Not that Dex himself was particularly impressed with what she could see. He was somewhat above average height but could not quite stretch far enough to tape six feet. He was a lean young man just shy of his twenty-ninth birthday, with dark blond hair and burnside whiskers worn all the way down onto the shelf of a square jaw. He had brown eyes, a face that women seemed to find more than passingly handsome and a smile that would melt the heart of any mother who had daughters of marriageable age.

Not that Dex was in the market for marriage. Play was more along his line than any of that sort of drudgery.

And play was what he did most thoroughly intend to do.

He held his arms out, and Candy came sliding into them.

Or anyway as close to him as she could manage with all that meat intruding between them.

Dex's ordinary preference was for sleek, lean, limber woman with long legs and narrow waists and a meager mouthful of tit to offer.

Candy Cane was . . . not in that mold. No sir, not hardly. In fact her tits were so big that it took some grabbing and hugging and reaching before a man might realize that she had thighs like tree trunks and a waist that would challenge a harness maker's skills just to cut a belt for her.

But her face was pretty, her mouth generous and . . . those tits. They made up for any amount of failings in other departments.

Dex lowered his head and gently suckled, first on one nipple and then the other.

Candy, incredibly enough, stiffened and then quickly cried out as he lightly bit into the hard, rubbery flesh of her left nipple.

"You didn't . . ."

"Sure I did. But jeez. Please. Don't stop now."

He went back to what he'd been doing, guiding her to a seat on the bed as he did so and then pressing her backward so that she lay beside him on the lumpy and none too fresh smelling bed. Not that he cared about such minor details as that. Not right then, he didn't.

Candy had, by actual count, four explosions before he shifted his attention away from her tits and began a slow exploration into the black bush that sprouted in the center of her crotch. He encountered moisture there. And more explosions. The girl was mighty easy to please.

"Here, honey." She tugged at him. "D'you want to fuck my tits first? A lot of fellows like that, and if you come there I'll lick the juice off." She was smiling. And it wasn't the sort of offer a boy received just every old day.

Dex smiled back at her. And raised himself over her body.

Such a lovely way to pass an evening, he was thinking as he lowered himself onto Candy's warm and willing flesh.

♦ 2 ♦

"Have a nice night of it?"

"Passing fair," Dex said with a grin. "How about you?"

James threw his head back and laughed. "You know the old saying, white boy. Try being a nigger just one Saturday night and you'll never want to go back to being white."

James was Dex's best friend. He was also black. Well, milk chocolate brown if not precisely black. When both were children James was given to Dexter as a slave and playtoy. Their friendship lasted long after the institution of slavery died. James was a year younger than Dex and was a hair taller but had the same unconsciously athletic build and even fairly similar features.

Once they left the Louisiana plantation they'd known all their lives—an event not entirely of their own choosing—one of the revelations of travel was their discovery that in the wide-open West a black man could be accepted with something close to equality. Here they could travel without the pretense that James was Dexter's servant. It was a freedom neither had expected.

"Hungry?"

"I could eat a mule," James said.

"Don't say that. You might jinx us. I dunno if you noticed the dining room of this place, but I wouldn't put it past them to serve mule meat in there. If it was cheap enough."

"You know what to do in that case."

Dex raised an eyebrow and waited.

"Don't ask," James concluded.

"Damn, I'm glad I can always count on you for sage advice."

"My pleasure, white boy. Any time at all."

"We could walk around and try to find a cleaner cafe or restaurant. There has to be one."

"Sure, why not."

They finished dressing, and Dex buckled on his brace of Webley revolvers, one worn in plain sight in a crossdraw rig at his belly, the other tucked away in the small of his back.

James carried a much lighter pair of break-top .32s in shoulder holsters worn under his coat.

In addition to the firearms, Dex customarily carried a cane with a very handsome eagle's-beak head. It wasn't that he needed any assistance walking, but he did like knowing he could rely on the slim, steel sword blade contained within the malacca barrel of his cane.

"Ready?"

"As I'll ever be."

They ambled down the stairs of the small town hotel and out into the sunshine of a bright and beautiful new day.

⬧ 3 ⬧

Breakfast was only fair. Dex might have rated it higher except these damn fools in ... wherever they were ... didn't know enough to add some fire-roasted chicory to their coffee beans. The brown water that passed for coffee here wasn't strong enough to put hair on a billygoat's chin. Back in Louisiana they knew how to make coffee. Now that was a fact.

Dex was intent on explaining all of this to James, who already knew it but was polite enough to listen anyway, when they were interrupted by a loud squeal from somewhere nearby.

"What was that?"

"Sounded like a woman hollering," James said.

The sound was repeated.

"The gentlemanly thing would be for us to go see if we can help," Dex said. "I think it came from right around the corner."

"Yes, and that's too close for comfort, white boy. The sensible thing would be for us to head back to that miserable little pissant hotel just as quick as we can run the distance."

"You, sir, are no gentleman."

"Us Negroes damn sure aren't and won't ever be. Times like this I'm glad that's so. Now c'mon, Dex. Don't go over there, I'm telling you."

But by then the advice was too late. It was being delivered to the back of Dex's head as Yancey legged it down the board sidewalk and around the corner into the next street.

The female voice screeched a third time as Dex turned into the side street and saw a young woman standing in the driving box of a light cabriolet. She held a buggy whip in one hand while the other clung to the back of the buggy's seat.

Standing beside the cabriolet was a tall man wearing a handsomely tailored suit, a diamond stickpin big enough to gag a buzzard and a scowl hot enough to crisp bacon at twenty paces.

As Dex approached this feuding pair the man reached as if to grab the driving lines of the buggy, and with another yelp the woman cut at him with the whip. The man was too close for the lash to reach him and needed to have no fear of the lightweight shaft, but a cut on his cheek that was bleeding into his beard showed that he'd already paid something of a price in order to come so close to the rig. The woman tried again to hit him with the whip but succeeded only in losing her balance and toppling over onto the seat cushions, her skirts flying high enough to reveal a slim and rather shapely ankle.

"Damn you, Elly," the man barked. "Come down off that seat and listen to what I have to say t' you."

"Leave me alone, Curtis. Just you go 'way and leave me alone." She tried again to whap him with the whip but with no better success than before. The man named Curtis grabbed the whip away from her and looked for a moment as if he intended to hit her with the thick buttstock.

Until that moment Dex had been undecided. Now that he saw what was going on he suspected the confrontation was probably a quarrel between a man and his missus. And a gentleman does not interfere with the way another man chooses to discipline his own.

Still, a gentleman does not stand idly by while a man takes a buggy whip to a woman, even if that woman is his wife.

Dex took three quick strides forward. His left hand flicked out and intercepted the strike of the whip handle before it connected with flesh.

"Not a good idea," he told the startled and newly enraged man who was so surprised that he relinquished his hold on the buggy whip.

"Ma'am," Dex said with a smile and a half bow, "is this gentleman your husband?"

"He is not, sir."

"Thank you, ma'am." Dex turned to the glowering fellow and admonished him. "I believe you owe the lady an apology, sir. You were carried away in the heat of the moment, I'm sure."

"Who the hell are you?" the tall gent demanded.

"Dexter Lee Yancey, sir, late of the great state of Louisiana." Dex allowed the soft, fluid accents of the deep South to broaden his voice. "And may I ask the same of you, sir?"

"I am . . . dammit, man, it doesn't matter who I am."

Dex continued to smile. "Since you are not this lady's husband, sir, I will conclude that you are correct. But given that fact, sir, I must tell you that I cannot stand by while you mistreat her so." He turned and placed the buggy whip firmly into the socket at the side of the cabriolet's dashboard.

As soon as Dex turned away from him the tall and rather powerfully built man saw his opportunity and struck out at Dex's unprotected back.

• 4 •

Ah, how perfidious humankind may often be! Not that Dex took time to ponder this sad fact. Nor did it come as any great surprise to him. In truth he'd been expecting something of the sort—after all, a man who would take a buggy whip to a woman not his wife was certainly no gentleman—and had turned his eyes away but not his attention.

The fellow's movements were shown in full detail by his shadow. And that lay within Dex's line of sight.

As soon as the man acted, Dex reacted.

Smaller but also younger, quicker and in much better physical condition than the tall man, Dex ducked under a blow that had been intended to land between his shoulder blades. He whirled and—his weight already balanced and in rapid motion—put his entire body behind a low left fist that sank wrist deep into the big man's belly just inches below his sternum.

There was a loud whoosh as air was driven from the fellow's lungs. The flesh visible above his beard went suddenly pale, and his mouth gaped like a catfish tossed onto the riverbank.

The man doubled over and gasped in an attempt to recapture the lost air. The posture presented a perfect opportunity. One small step backward and a good, hard kick would permanently rearrange the shape of the fellow's face.

That sort of thing, though, was serious and only undertaken when there was a genuine desire to cause harm. It wasn't for this kind of street encounter with a stranger.

Dex let the moment pass and stood aside while the big man dropped to his knees and liberally fertilized the street with whatever he'd eaten over the past two or three days. Dex couldn't help but notice that the fellow ate very well, or at least ate in great quantity. It took him quite a long time to unburden himself of it all.

Dex became bored—and more than a little queasy—with watching this rather unpleasant display so after only a few moments he turned his attention back to the lady. He doffed his hat and bowed very slightly. "Miss."

"Thank you, sir. I am in your debt."

"Not at all. I am only sorry that you were troubled. I . . ."

The words remained unspoken, interrupted by another piercing shriek of terror from the lady.

Dex whirled again.

The woman's scream was punctuated by the sharp, brittle report of a small caliber revolver, and a gout of dirt and vomit leaped off the surface of the street and sprayed both the ground nearby and the trousers of the man who was kneeling on the ground there.

The big man looked wildly about to see James standing at the street corner with one of his .32s in hand, a wisp of smoke rising from its muzzle.

The fellow blanched and with very great care laid a very small, nickel-plated pocket pistol onto the ground.

Apparently he'd had every intention of shooting Dexter in the back.

"You should be ashamed of yourself," Dex said to him. "Slide that little thing over here, will you. We wouldn't want to burden you with more temptation, now would we."

The man gave Dex a glare that would have put him six feet under if only looks could kill. But he did as he was instructed and tossed the little gun closer to Dex's boots.

Dex retrieved the pistol and dropped it into his own

pocket. He stood over the man for a moment, assessing both the person and the situation.

No, he thought. This was not a nice man. A woman-beater and a back-shooter and God knew what else. It was all such a shame.

Dex sighed.

And kicked the son of a bitch in the face so hard it sent him flying hard onto his back with his nose flattened, probably with his jaw broken and most certainly with his entire head and upper body soon to be drenched in the flow of his own blood.

"Manners," Dex said in a deceptively mild tone. "We must remember our manners, sir."

From behind him he heard a sharp whistle and the crunch of iron tire rims on gravel as the woman spanked her team into motion, obviously wanting the hell out of there and never mind the pleasantries.

Not that Dex could blame her. He watched the cabriolet speed away and make a turn out of sight at the next corner.

The well-dressed fellow who was no gentleman still lay sprawled in the street amid blood and dirt and his own puke.

Townspeople were beginning to show themselves now that the shouting and the shooting were over. Dex decided it was probably safe to walk away.

But he kept an eye on the SOB anyway until he'd reached the street corner close to the cafe and was able to put the solid and comforting presence of a building between himself and the big man.

• 5 •

"Nice shooting back there, James. Thanks."

"I was aiming at the man, actually."

"Oh. In that case . . ." Dex just grinned.

"Can I make a suggestion?" James asked.

"Of course. You do understand, I hope, that I'll most likely ignore it. But suggest away."

"I think we oughta get the hell outa this town, Dexter. Like . . . right now?"

"Y'know, James, there are times when even an ugly ol' black boy like you comes up with a good idea. I agree with you."

"Good." James lengthened his stride, and Dex had to hurry some to keep up with him.

They went back to the hotel and upstairs to begin what little packing was necessary. Traveling by horseback as they'd been doing for some time now meant traveling very light. A pair of saddlebags apiece. A few articles of clothing wrapped in a sausagelike roll and tied behind their cantles. That was about the size of it. Well, that and the money belt that James wore, James being in charge of their wherewithal on the theory that a highwayman was very apt to shake Dexter down but would not so likely suspect the gentleman's black "servant" of having anything of value on his person.

Dex fingered his chin. He hadn't had a shave in two days and had really been looking forward to a visit to a barber after breakfast. It seemed that would have to wait until they reached the next town. Whenever and wherever that proved to be.

"Do you have enough in your pocket to take care of the hotel bill and the stable charges?" James asked.

"Plenty, thanks." Dex buckled closed the leather flaps of his saddlebags and tossed them onto the lone chair in the room. He was laying the square of rubberized cloth out on the bed ready to complete his packing when there was a knock at the door.

"Who is it?"

"Town marshal, Mr. Yancey."

Dex looked at James and mouthed a silent but heartfelt, "Shit." Aloud he said, "Just a minute."

With a shrug and an air of resignation he went to the door and slid the bolt back. The voice did not sound like that of the big man he'd left in the street back there. But then a fellow never knew what sort of friends a man might have. When he pulled the door open a crack Dex was standing well clear of it. Just in case.

There were, in fact, no wild-eyed attackers lurking in the hallway, only a middle-aged man with a spreading paunch and a much younger fellow who was overdue for a haircut.

"May we come in, sir?"

"Yes, of course."

The older man stepped in and to the side. His deputy joined him and posted himself immediately in front of the door, effectively if unobtrusively blocking the way if anyone decided to bolt.

"I am Tom Harris, Mr. Yancey. I'm town marshal of Winter Grove. This is my deputy, Henry Langley."

"It seems you already know who I am."

"Yes, sir. I took the liberty of looking at the guest register downstairs."

"And how may I help you, Marshal?"

"It's about that assault in the street a little while ago, sir. A very serious affair, I'm told. Assault with a deadly weapon. Intent to kill. Perhaps other charges, but I'll let the prosecuting attorney and the judge iron all that out. My job is only to make the arrest and see to the well-being of the prisoner, thank goodness. I don't have a head for all that other stuff."

Dex looked at the portly town marshal with his straggly mustache and cigar ash stains on his vest. The man wore no badge, at least none that was visible. And he had a folksy, aw-shucks appearance.

It was an impression that Dex did not for one moment believe. Since he'd entered the room his eyes were in constant motion, taking in every detail. And his deputy, although making no more of a show of himself than the marshal did, was positioned perfectly and without need for instruction.

No, Dex decided, these two knew exactly what they were about. Dex had no doubt at all that they would be formidable opponents in a scrap.

Not that it should come to that. The facts were simple enough, and simple truth would take care of this situation.

With any kind of luck their departure would be delayed by only a matter of hours. Say, a day or two at the very worst.

Dex nodded and smiled at Harris. "No problem, Marshal. Will you want to handcuff me or will you accept my parole to go along willingly?"

"Sir?"

"I asked . . ."

"Oh, I heard what you said well enough, Mr. Yancey, but it isn't you I've come here for. It's your nigger there that I have to put under arrest. He tried to kill a man this morning, you know."

◆ 6 ◆

The Winter Grove jail was housed in a most unimpressive wooden annex built as an add-on wing to the town hall. Dex had no particular expertise when it came to jails, but he suspected this one would be a snap to fetch James out of if things should come to that. After all, those light clapboards would pull loose with a quick tug on a crowbar. A little screech of nails coming free, a few minutes of effort and a man could step right through the newly created gap in the wall.

Unimpressive, Dex thought. Until they went inside.

Oh, the building was flimsy enough. The wall could be taken apart just as easily as Dex first thought.

But there wouldn't be much point to the exercise.

Turned out the whole damned building could be dismantled without having any effect on the containment of prisoners.

Inside there were a pair of desks, some armchairs, one rocking chair, a rifle rack, set of filing cabinets, oversized potbelly stove, and two jail cells. The cells were fabricated of iron-bar sections that very obviously had been bought elsewhere—probably they were a patented design available to towns by mail order—and freighted to Winter Grove in pieces ready for convenient assembly inside the wooden building.

Each section looked to be about eight feet tall and six feet wide. The two cells were each one section wide and two deep, making the cell dimensions roughly six feet by twelve. The front panels had doors built in, each with a small pass-through where plates of food or other small articles could be exchanged without having to unlock the doors.

A barred ceiling had been created by placing more panels overhead, and the floor was made of spot-welded steel sheets.

Dex was impressed. The jail here was much nicer—and much more secure—than anything they had back home.

Both cells were empty when Marshal Harris took James in with Dex and Deputy Langley trailing behind. Each cell held a pair of metal bunks stacked one above the other, and each had a steel bucket placed in a corner in lieu of a thundermug. Another bucket was placed in front of the divider where prisoners in either cell could reach through the bars for a dipper if they were thirsty. The cell bunks had neither mattresses nor springs, just sheet-steel beds to lie on. Each bunk also had a blanket neatly folded and ready for use. No pillows, though.

No mattress, no pillow, no comfort.

All in all, Dex thought, the cells were efficient . . . and damned well depressing. He didn't envy James the time he would have to spend locked inside one.

"Mr. Yancey, you can sit over there, if you please." Harris pointed to a chair at the side of the office. "You sit there," he said to James, this time indicating one of the chairs in front of his desk.

"I'll need for you to turn over everything that's in your pockets. Hand everything to Langley and state out loud what it is you're giving to him. Slow, if you please. I'll be writing it all down, you see. We'll make an inventory of your things, put everything into a poke and lock it up. I will sign the inventory on behalf of the town, and you'll either sign or make your mark to show you agree with the list. You with me about this? All right, good. When you're released, if you're released, you'll get it all back. If you're transferred to state custody and on to the penitentiary everything will be turned over to them, and you'll get another list. D'you understand all that, boy?"

"Yessuh, I does, suh." James had gone into his mushmouth, po' ol' nigra routine, Dex saw. "Yessuh, I sho'ly does."

"That's fine. Henry, you can take the handcuffs off him now." Harris looked at James and smiled. "You might want to sit quiet now. You wouldn't want us to think you were trying to run."

"Nossuh, bawss, I wouldn' do lak that, suh."

"No, I'm sure you would not. And by the way, boy. No need for you to bother with the cornpone crap. I've already asked about you, and I know you aren't some woodpile nigger. They say you talk just like a white man."

James grinned at him. "As you wish, Marshal Harris."

"Thank you, boy. I appreciate your cooperation. Smartasses don't impress me, black nor white." The marshal cocked an eye across the room toward Dex. "You sit nice and quiet over there too if you please, Mr. Yancey."

"Of course."

"May I ask a question, sir?" James put in.

"Go ahead."

"May I give some of the things on my person to Mr. Yancey for safekeeping, sir?"

"No, that would be against our rules."

"I'm wearing a money belt, sir. The money is his. I've been carrying it for him. It wouldn't be right for his money to be locked up."

"Sorry. We have rules here, and we follow them."

Dex winced. He hadn't thought about that, dammit. Not that it should matter much. After all, James would only be here briefly. A matter of hours if they were lucky, a day or so at the most.

"Now if we can get on with this." He withdrew a printed form from a desk drawer and brought out a set of pens and a bottle of prepared ink. "What is your name, boy?"

• 7 •

Dex looked at his friend. James seemed thoroughly miserable inside the cell. Well, there wasn't anything odd about that. Anyone would be. The problem now would be to get him out again. Fast.

"May I ask your advice about a few things, Sheriff?"

"I'm only a town marshal, Mr. Yancey, as I suspect you caught well enough the first time." Harris smiled. "But there's no harm in spreading a dab of butter on things. Feel free to call me 'your excellency' if you like. Nobody's ever tried that one so far."

This was not an occasion for levity, but Dex found himself liking the marshal despite it all. The man was not unpleasant in the slightest. Merely . . . professional. To a fault.

"First thing you should know," Harris said, "is about visiting hours. You're allowed to visit in the evenings only. We feed our prisoners about five. You're welcome to visit between six and eight. But don't bother me any earlier and don't expect to stay any later.

"I'm here myself until six every day, rain or shine, weekday or weekend, I'm here to six. My night man takes over then. His name is Emmett Tyler, and you should know that Emmett wouldn't bend a rule for God Almighty unless I said it was all right. So do us all a favor, yourself included, and don't ask to pass anything from your hand to the prisoner's and don't ask to stay later than eight. It won't matter to me or to Emmett if you're smack in the middle of the most serious game of checkers that's ever been played, come eight o'clock you walk outa here. D'we understand each other, Mr. Yancey?"

"We do, Marshal. Now as to my next question?" Not that he'd had a chance to ask the first yet. But in truth Harris had correctly anticipated what that would have been.

"Yes indeed, sir."

"We'll be needing the services of a lawyer, I believe. Do your rules permit you to recommend one?"

"Not only am I allowed to do that, Mr. Yancey, it's very easily done. You see, we have only one lawyer residing in Winter Grove. His name is Blake. C. J. Blake."

"That does simplify matters," Dex agreed. "Have you any idea where I could find him, sir?"

"I do indeed. At the moment I believe he is over at Doc Stuart's office having his teeth and jaw attended to. Last I heard Doc didn't know if the jaw was busted or if Curtis would get by with only losing some teeth."

"You don't mean . . . ?"

Harris smiled and spread his hands. "When it rains, Mr. Yancey, it does sometimes pour. Seems our one and only town lawyer is the same gentleman your boy tried to kill this morning."

Back in his jail cell James turned damn near pale when he heard that.

The news didn't do much for Dex's state of mind either.

• 8 •

The storekeeper adjusted his spectacles, squinted and tilted his head toward the daylight coming through his shop window, then removed the spectacles and spent some time carefully and slowly polishing each lens before he looked toward Dexter. He replaced the glasses onto his face one wire earpiece at a time. Finally he spoke. "Young woman, you say. Big bonnet. Nice dress. Driving a cabriolet and name of Elly. The lady, I mean, not the buggy, ha ha." He hiccuped and gave Dex a rather odd look before he said, "Yes, I expect I know who that would be."

Dex waited but the man looked down toward the ledger on his counter and acted as if he had no intention of adding anything to the admission.

"Well?" Dex asked, careful to keep any impatience from his voice.

"Well what?"

"You said you know her. Well?"

"I said that, so I did." The shopkeeper looked absently off into the distance. "Say now, mister, were you wanting to buy anything?"

Ah. So that was the game. Hardly subtle, but . . . "That's what I came in to do, yes, but I thought I'd talk to you for a few moments before I do my shopping." The man sold an assortment of hardware items, rather shoddy looking off-the-shelf clothing and small notions. Dex doubted he could find anything of use to him here if he examined each and every item in the place.

"Yes, well, um, if you want to find the woman, she lives straight west from town 'bout a quarter mile. Her house is back of a stand of poplar trees. Tall house. White. You can't miss it."

"And the lady's name?"

"Adams," the storekeeper said. "Miz Eleanor Adams. Widow woman, she is. Came from back East someplace and married Ned Adams. Anything else you want to know?"

"No, sir, thank you." Dex turned and headed for the door.

"Hey. Mister!"

"Yes?"

"I thought you was gonna do some shopping."

"Oh, I am. I surely am. But I just thought of something I have to do first. I'll be back. Count on it."

Dex gave the semihelpful fellow a bright and cheery smile, then hurried off toward the hotel where his and James's horses were quartered in a small barn behind the place. He'd already learned that some people, town dwellers in particular, have very strange notions of distance and a quarter mile to one might be the same as a mile and a quarter to someone else, and he had no intention of walking the maybe-quarter mile out to the Widow Adams's house.

House, the man had said, and house it most certainly was. The fellow at the store back in town—a distance that Dex judged to be almost exactly a quarter mile behind him—just hadn't mentioned what *sort* of house the widow lady occupied.

This house, screened by a windbreak stand of poplar trees on the north and west sides, showed heavy, scarlet red draperies that completely covered the windows, and there was a lantern mounted permanently on either side of the front door. The glass panes in the lanterns were as red as blood.

The front porch was devoid of the rocking chairs one might normally expect to find there. But then gentlemen in even the most relaxed and accommodating of communities do not generally socialize outdoors when visiting in a house of this sort.

A graveled drive led around the south side of the house to a small wagon park and a long line of hitching posts. Apparently business in this location could be good.

Nearby was a shed where the cabriolet was parked under cover and beyond that was a pen with several horses in it, one of them the animal that Mrs. Adams was driving earlier. He'd come to the right place, all right.

But it didn't seem likely that . . .

Well hell, he didn't know anything about Winter Grove or Mrs. Eleanor Adams or much of anything else around here. The one thing he knew for sure was that he wanted to get himself and James the hell away from this place.

Dex made sure his horse was securely tied, then tugged and tucked at his clothes before he walked around to the front of the place and mounted the steps onto the porch of the whorehouse.

His rapping on the door brought—eventually—a very small and very annoyed young black woman to the door.

"Go 'way, mister. We ain't open this early. You come back tonight sometime. You come back after supper. We be open then."

"I just want to talk to, uh, one of the ladies who works . . . I mean to say, I need to speak with someone who . . ."

The black woman sniffed loudly and shut the door in his face.

"Dammit," Dex mumbled.

He reached out and tapped on the door again.

When that brought no response he tried the heavy brass knocker. And again. And then very loudly.

The door was snatched open. "Mister, you hush that crap or you wake all the ladies."

"Sorry. I only need to wake one of them. She is . . ."

"It's all right, Betty Lou. Ask the gentleman in, if you please."

Betty Lou looked behind her with considerable surprise. But she did as she was instructed.

Dex removed his hat before stepping indoors. He passed through the vestibule to a gaudily ornate foyer. Off to the left was an even more blatantly gaudy parlor and to the right a piano room. A staircase led to what would surely be the "business" section of the establishment. The Widow Adams stood at the foot of the stairs.

"Nice to see you again, Mr. Yancey."

"My pleasure, ma'am." He bowed and made a leg, treating her with all the courtesy possible. After all, it was a wise man indeed who first framed the expression: Treat a lady like a whore and a whore like a lady. Each seemed to like being so handled.

"Betty Lou. Bring tea and a tray of sweets to my office, please."

"Yessum." The black girl bobbed her head and hurried away.

Dex followed Mrs. Adams through the piano room and to the back of the house where what might have been intended as a pantry or storage area had been turned into a small but elegantly furnished office. The furniture was Queen Anne style, very delicate and pretty. On the walls were paintings of ladies-in-waiting with courtiers laughing and chatting in the background and the buxom ladies being attended by apple-cheeked little boys in silk breeches and lace. Dex gave several of them—there were five in all—a close look but did not recognize the scrawled signature, which was the same on both paintings that he looked at.

"Do you know art, Mr. Yancey?"

"Know it? I do not. But I like it very much."

"And do you like these pieces?"

"I do, ma'am." That was an exaggeration but only a very small one. His own personal taste ran more toward horses and hounds than ladies-in-waiting, but he did rather like the artist's sense of composition and color. And said so.

"Thank you, Mr. Yancey. You've quite made my day." She smiled. "Twice, actually."

"You painted these?"

She dropped her eyes modestly. "I did, sir. It was once my dream to become an artist. That was before I learned that only men can be valued as true artists."

"Pardon me? Who was it wrote that rule?" he asked.

"Virtually every gallery owner and art critic in this country or any other. Can you name an exception? I daresay you cannot."

Dex paused and thought and . . . indeed could not. Every one of the masters, every single painter or sculptor he'd ever heard of, was male. "You're right. Damn me if you aren't," he said after several long moments of thinking back to his school days and all the reading he'd done since.

"Exactly," she said, then pointed to a rather insubstantial-looking chair while she herself settled gracefully into a much more comfortable looking seat behind the desk.

"Before you get to the business that brought you here, Mr. Yancey, may I ask you something?"

"Of course."

"When you announced yourself this morning, you mentioned your full name. Do you happen to be related to the Lees of Virginia? *The* Lees, I mean?"

"To Lighthorse Harry Lee and to Marse Robert? Yes, on my mother's side. She was something like a fourth cousin to the general. Of course to her he was just Cousin Bobby, or so I'm told. She died long before Cousin Bobby became so well-known. It was Lighthorse Harry who was the focus of family lore and pride until then. Not that I ever met either of them, you understand. My mother died early, and while I've met a few of the Virginia cousins and some in the Carolinas I was raised a Yancey in Louisiana."

"But as a true Southern gentleman of taste and breeding, I gather," Mrs. Adams prompted.

"I like to think so, yes. Why do you ask?"

She shrugged. "It isn't important. May I ask what brought you here, Mr. Yancey? I believe you've already been told we do not normally accommodate patrons until evening. But I suppose we could make an exception if you wish to, shall we say, receive compensation for your gallantry this morning. I could have Betty Lou wake one of my ladies if you like."

"Having seen the beauty of their employer, ma'am, I am sure I could never be satisfied with any of your ladies." He inclined his head in a miniature bow.

And in truth, Eleanor Adams was quite pretty. Her hair was a rich shade of auburn piled and pinned quite properly, and her skin had no need of the artifices of powder or rouge. He judged her to be still in her twenties, young enough that her flesh had that taut, smooth, elasticity that cannot be faked. Nor retained past its time.

She had pale eyes—gray, he thought although he might have been mistaken about that—and a slender neck.

She'd changed clothing after her morning drive into town and was now wearing a full-cut dress that concealed her figure. Even so she was a remarkably young and pretty woman.

Dex couldn't help but wonder if Mrs. Adams entertained customers upstairs. That wasn't what was offered to him. But if it had been he would have been happy to take her up on it.

"That was not the reason I came, ma'am. I've come to ask for your help with another matter although it does relate to the, um, incident with Mr. Blake this morning. May I explain?"

He waited for her nod, then launched into the tale about James and his need for testimony. They were interrupted by Betty Lou's arrival with the tea and a silver tray of sweetmeats, but Mrs. Adams listened carefully to what Dex had to say.

She was frowning by the time he concluded.

· 10 ·

"I'm sorry, Mr. Yancey."

"You won't testify?" He was surprised. He'd thought the woman rather nice, never mind her choice of occupation.

"It isn't that I would be unwilling," she said. "Only that my testimony would not help in this matter. Far from it, actually. If I were to appear on a witness stand it would only solidify the jurors against him. Think about it. A whoremonger and a nigra conspiring together to damage one of the community's leading citizens. You don't know the people here but believe me. My testimony would as good as guarantee a verdict against your man. A jury here wouldn't believe a single word either one of us said."

"How did you know James is colored?" Dex asked, suddenly suspicious.

"I was there this morning, remember? I saw him."

"Oh, I . . . forgot."

"You are upset, Mr. Yancey. Distracted."

"Yes, I suppose so." He sighed, feeling helpless and very frustrated now that his primary line of defense seemed to have been dashed to pieces on the shoals of reality. "I don't know . . ." Hell, he didn't even know how to finish that simple sentence. He didn't know jack shit, that's what he didn't know.

"It may be to your advantage, Mr. Yancey, for you to simply go on. You can hire another servant. And your man won't be mistreated in jail here. Marshal Harris will be scrupulously fair. He'll be put to work doing odd jobs around town. Raking the streets and filling ruts, repairing sidewalks, things like that. It won't be bad. And how long can the sentence be? A few months probably. When his time has been served Marshal Harris will give him a dollar and a coach ticket out of town. He'll be fine. And in the meantime you can be on about your business."

"You don't understand. James isn't my servant. He's my friend."

The woman's eyes brows lifted. Then she shrugged. "I see." She tipped her head to one side for a moment while she studied him, then shrugged a second time. "I wouldn't have guessed."

"Wouldn't have guessed what?"

"That you and the nigra are, shall we say, a couple."

Dex threw his head back and roared. "Good Lord. Wait until I tell James that one."

"Am I missing something here?"

Dex grinned at her. "No indeed, ma'am. You have me pegged absolutely right. But I think if you want to do your Christian duty . . . charity, you could call it . . . you could try to cure me of my, uh, problem. You know. Convince me that I can find true happiness with a member of the fair sex. A person never knows until he tries. So why don't you take me upstairs and see if you can get me to perform. Show me how to do it. I promise I'll try my best. I only ask you to be . . . gentle with me. And teach me what to do."

Eleanor Adams laughed. "All right. So I was wrong."

"No, no, not at all. Really. But I think you could cure me. Please tell me you'll try."

"You're a very handsome gentleman, Mr. Yancey, and the real thing. A true gentleman of the South. If I were ever tempted to take a man up those stairs it would be you. As it happens, however, my policy is that I never, ever compete with my ladies for the attentions of our patrons. That would be greedy and stupid and bad for business. So I shall most regretfully decline your suggestion."

Dex shook his head. "In that case I may be trapped in a life of abomination forever. And it will be all your fault."

"We will both have to live with that, won't we."

"Look, is there any way you can think of for me to get justice here?" Dex asked, returning to the original point of his visit. "Tell me about the local situation, please."

Eleanor too sobered. She steepled her fingertips and peered into the void between her palms for a moment before she spoke again. "I already mentioned that Marshal Harris is an honest man. Very correct. He finds the law always to be a matter of solid black and pure white. He doesn't allow for areas of grayness and will follow the law to the last little detail. That is good most of the time but not always."

Dex grunted.

"We have a municipal judge. A justice of the peace if you want to be formal about it. His appointment is from the county, which gives him jurisdiction over town matters and any other minor legal matters within a radius of ten miles or so around town. The county seat is almost thirty miles from here, so it is much easier if things can be handled in Winter Grove. Judge Grassley hears everything but the most serious cases.

"The thing you want to know about Herb Grassley is that he is not a lawyer and has no formal training in the law. He does have a book of common law . . . he bought it by mail order . . . and he likes to study his book whenever something new comes up. But to tell you the truth, I don't think he understands half of what he reads there. He's the town butcher by trade and took on the JP appointment so he could pick up a little extra money from fees. Mostly he marries people and signs birth certificates and notarizes bills of sale. Things like that. The town pays him a dollar a day for sitting on the bench so he's always eager to hear a motion. The thing you and your friend have to worry about is that Herb knows he isn't versed in the law, and he believes almost anything that son of a bitch Curtis tells him about law and precedent.

"Which brings us to Curtis. I don't know how good he is as a lawyer, but as a man he is one mean, conniving SOB. And I suspect he makes up half the things he tells Herb about legal precedent because the cases he cites are always in favor of whatever it is that Curtis wants. Curtis likes to think of himself as the big man around here, and he has designs on becoming still bigger. But then you already know you can't trust him. After all, he's the one who pulled a gun first this morning."

"I still have that pistol," Dex said. "I wonder if we could use that to prove that James was defending me."

"Perhaps," Eleanor said. "But you would have to have the trial moved to Connor and heard by a real judge over there. And to do that you would have to get Herb to relinquish jurisdiction. I don't think he would agree to that if Curtis didn't want him to."

"You seem to have a good grip on the people and situations around here, Mrs. Adams."

"I should. Most of these men are regular customers of mine."

"I see."

"Except for Marshal Harris. I like him and respect him, and I wouldn't want you to have a wrong impression about him. Marshal Harris is married, and he seems to take his marriage vows as seriously as he regards the law and his duties. The only times he comes here is when he tries to pump me for information, like to see if my girls have heard anything if there has been a crime. Things like that."

Dex knew better than to ask if she passed such information. Besides, he suspected he already knew the answer. He was pretty sure that she would. After all, she would want to retain the goodwill of a man who could probably shut her whorehouse down if he so chose. And asking her about it would only force her to lie to him. That would be pointless.

"I don't mean to pry," Dex said, knowing good and well

that that was the sort of thing a person said when they intended to damn well pry, "but that difficulty you were having with Curtis Blake this morning . . . was there anything about that that might effect James's and my situation?"

"I don't think so, Mr. Yancey."

"Then of course I shall accept your judgment on the subject and ask no more." He finished the tea that had grown cold while they talked and set the empty cup onto the front edge of the desk.

"Mr. Yancey."

"Yes, Mrs. Adams?"

"I truly am grateful to you for coming to my rescue this morning. If there is any way I can help you and your friend, I will be happy to do so."

"Thank you." He grinned. "There is that cure we talked about . . ."

But the notion brought only a laugh from the pretty madam. Darn it!

Dex stood and made his good-byes, treating the woman with all the courtesy that he would have given to the finest gentlelady in Louisiana.

When he left he had the sense that he knew much more now than he had when he arrived. And that none of that newfound knowledge was going to be the least bit helpful.

· 11 ·

"**I** thought I told you already that visiting hours aren't until after dinner," the Winter Grove marshal said in a none-too-patient tone.

"I didn't come to see him, Marshal. I came to talk with you."

"Mm, all right then. Have a seat." Harris laid his pen aside, carefully closed the folder he'd been working in and deposited it in a lower drawer. He cleaned his pen, capped the ink bottle and tidied the few papers visible on top of the desk. Only then did he give his attention to Dexter.

Far from being annoyed by the display of fussiness, Dex was pleased. Apparently when Tom Harris did grant his attention to someone or something it was total. He did not permit distractions. Dex rather liked that.

"I've been told, Marshal, that you are an honest man. I know James has told you what happened out there this morning. So have I. So will Mrs. Adams, I believe, if you care to ask her."

"Oh, I'll ask her. You can count on that. But I hope you understand the, um, problems that would be raised if she were to testify about what happened."

"I do, sir, and that's why I want to ask your advice,

Marshal. Speaking frankly, is there any likelihood we can have the charges against James dropped?"

"Very little, I would think. Almost nonexistent, in fact. Mr. Blake is . . . highly upset. Boiling mad, in fact. I don't think there is a snowball's chance of him dropping those charges."

"But I'm the one that broke his jaw. If it's broken, that is."

"It is. Doc told me that a little while ago. He's had to tie it up. Figures it will be the better part of two months before Blake can eat a solid meal again."

"I can't say that I'm disappointed to hear that, Marshal. But let me ask you something. You and I both know that I'm the one who broke his damn jaw. So why is James the one who has to pay the price for it?"

"You want the truth, Mr. Yancey? I'll give it to you. Curtis Blake can be a vindictive man. But he's also a realist. He knows good and well that if he tries to take you to trial, you'll ask for a jury trial instead of trusting Judge Grassley with the verdict. Most any man would under the circumstances, and you being a stranger in town, well, you can see the implications there."

"Yes sir, I can."

"So you'd ask for a jury, and you'd be entitled to that. Now even if it was only your word against his, what with neither Elly Adams nor your nigger being able to offer respectable testimony, a jury would see easy enough that what happened out there was a fair fight and that you won it. Curtis wouldn't likely win that contest. Worse, he'd be seen by this town as a poor loser in a fair fight. Folks wouldn't like that. It would hurt the man's reputation, and he wouldn't want that. Not for anything. He's an ambitious man, Curtis Blake is, and he wouldn't want to allow something personal, not even a busted jaw, to get in the way of that. I don't know what-all his plans are, but it's plain for all to see that he has them.

"But all that being true, it's a whole different story with your boy there. Folks here will look different at the idea of a nigger shooting at a white man. They won't like that, and

Curtis knows it. Elly Adams can't testify to any of it, not that anyone would listen. If she tried to say anything it would only piss people off, the idea of a whore taking up for a nigger. You see what I mean?"

Dex nodded.

"You'd testify for him, of course. Blake knows that. He also knows his neighbors. Doesn't matter who's on the jury. They'll look at your nigger and think about how he's yours, servant to some stranger passing through and of course you'd want to get him off. They don't know you to decide if you'd lie to keep your boy outa jail. What's more, they'd already know that you and Blake fought and that you broke his jaw. By now everyone in town already knows that much. Come tomorrow morning half the county will know it. So folks will figure you got a bone to pick with Blake anyway. That plus the fact that the boy is yours . . .

"Mr. Yancey I don't think there's much doubt why Curtis chose to file his charge against the nigger. It's the easiest way for him to get something back at you. Got damn little to do with the nigger himself. This is mostly a needle in your side, Mr. Yancey. And my advice to you this afternoon is the exact same as it was this morning. Leave that boy behind and go on about your business.

"You've said the two of you are friends? Fine. Tell him where he can meet up with you. Five, six months from now I'll turn him loose and give him a dollar and a stage ticket the same as I would a white man. You have my word on that. And there won't anything bad happen to him while he's in my jail. He'll eat as good as anybody else and he'll work like anybody else, and there won't any harm come to him. That's the way I run things. Count on it. So you just tell him where you'll meet him and be on your way. It'll turn out easier on everybody if you do that. Curtis Blake will get his pound of flesh . . . or half a pound is more like it, but he'll settle for the half. Your boy will spend a few months working for the public good. And there won't be any further harm done to anybody." Harris paused. "It's good advice, Mr. Yancey. I truly hope you will take it."

"Thank you for your time, Marshal. And thank you for your honesty."

"Any time, Mr. Yancey, any time."

Dex sent a sorrowful look toward James but left without speaking to him. Marshal Harris deserved that much co-operation, he thought, and James would understand.

· 12 ·

Connor wasn't much larger than Winter Grove but it had a railroad spur and set of feedlots on the north side, and Dex supposed that was reason enough why Connor was county seat and Winter Grove was not.

The town was built around a square that proudly featured a narrow, boxy, three-story tall courthouse built of sandstone. Dex let his horse water at one of the public troughs that had been placed on each side of the square, then tied the animal at a nearby rail and mounted the marble steps of the courthouse.

"There is no point in you bothering the judge, mister," a clerk told him when he'd stated his business. "A third party can't apply for a change of venue. Your partner's lawyer can file a motion about that, but the motion will have to be heard by Judge Grassley over there. Judge Wiggin wouldn't consider it until Judge Grassley has entered a ruling. Wouldn't be proper. That's official. If you want some unofficial information as a free of charge extra, mister, I can tell you something else. Judge Wiggin won't overrule Judge Grassley unless there is powerful reason for him to.

"You may not want to hear this, mister, but it's gospel.

It isn't Judge Wiggin you want to see. It's a lawyer. They got a lawyer right over there in Winter Grove. Name of Blake. Julian Blake. You look him up. I shouldn't say this but you look like a nice fella . . . lay out whatever Blake asks for a fee and you won't have any trouble getting your change of venue. Everybody around here knows that Judge Grassley agrees with pretty much anything Julian Blake wants from him. You know what I mean?"

"I know, all right," Dex said. "Are there any lawyers here in Connor I could talk to?"

The clerk gave him a look of mild annoyance at Dex's apparent failure to appreciate such good advice freely offered, but he did answer the question. "Got three to choose from. Hadlock and Parker deal in civil matters. Land titles, business filings, like that. Their offices are across the street next door to the bank. Gus Roberts does mostly criminal work. He has an office two blocks down in that direction," he pointed, "but you won't likely find him there. He's in court today. Second floor. If you want to talk to him instead of Mr. Blake, you can go up and wait for them to finish for the day. It's, what?" The clerk squinted and looked at a large Regulator clock on the wall. "Twelve minutes past three. Judge Wiggin likes to stop before four on Wednesdays." He grinned. "Bridge and brandy with his pals every Wednesday night while the wives are out at church for Bible study, don't you see. They like to get started just as quick as the ladies walk out the door so court never runs late on a Wednesday."

Dex thanked the man and found the staircase—ordinary sandstone that was already wearing down instead of the flashier but more expensive marble on display outside—and resigned himself to waiting for a chance to talk with this Gus Roberts.

• 13 •

Dex glanced toward the sun when he stepped outside. There were dark clouds looming in the west, and it looked like rain would be coming sooner or later.

It was a good six-hour ride back to Winter Grove and that was if he chose to push the horse. Apart from the fact that he had no desire to make that ride twice in one day—first coming to Connor and the next time leaving it—he most assuredly did not want to do it in the rain. Better, he decided, to take a room here for the night and head back to Winter Grove in the morning.

After all, it wasn't like he had any good news to convey to James.

He'd found the lawyer Roberts easily enough, but the son of a bitch was more interested in getting a quick supper before his card game than in making himself helpful.

No, he did not practice in Winter Grove, he'd said. Too damn far.

No, he would not file a motion before Judge Grassley, he'd said. Too damn ignorant.

No, he would not invite himself into a butt-kicking contest with Curtis Blake, he'd said. Too damn mean.

The upshot of all Dex's posturing and pleading had been

that Gus Roberts went placidly along toward his damned card game while Dex went fuming and growling in search of a place to stay overnight.

"You look like you've had a bad day, friend," the desk clerk at the Excelsior Resort and Inn sympathized.

"Mister, you don't know the half of it," Dex agreed.

"How long will you be with us, sir?"

"Just for tonight."

"Very good, sir." The clerk produced a canvas bound ledger, opened it to a bookmarked page that was about a third full and turned it so Dex could sign in. "That will be five dollars, sir."

"Five . . . ? Mister, I only want to stay the one night, I said."

"Yes, I heard you. Five dollars for one night. Thirty for the full week."

"Isn't that awful high?"

"Not at all, sir. Our room rate includes use of the hot springs and mud baths."

"But all I want is a place to sleep. I don't intend to use hot springs or mud baths." The idea of wallowing in hot mud like a boar hog in shit sounded remarkably unappealing.

"That would be your choice, sir. The rate is five dollars regardless. Do you want the room or not?"

This visit to Connor was *not* going the way Dex had hoped.

"Not," he said.

The desk clerk closed his handsome ledger and put it out of sight under the counter. "Perhaps another time, sir."

"Yeah. Right." Dex turned and stalked away, his mood none the better after this little visit.

And he still didn't have a place to stay, dammit.

· 14 ·

Dex drank off half of his beer, his humor even more bitter than the poor quality brew he'd been served.

Things in this town started badly and were only getting worse. The man at the livery pointed him to a reasonably priced hotel with no trouble. Then promptly warned that all beds had to be shared. With humans usually and with bedbugs always.

Neither thought was appealing. Dex concluded he would be better off sleeping in the livery barn hayloft than in a vermin-filled bed. He'd heard that sort of thing was an accepted practice out in this very uncivilized West. He'd never had to resort to it before, but he supposed there was always a first time for everything. Or so the old saying contended. Miserable damned old saying!

He took another swallow of his beer and reached for a slice of the thin and overly dry pink stuff that passed for ham on the free lunch tray.

Instead of ham he took hold of a hand.

"Sorry," he said, turning to see who it was he'd grasped.

"No harm done, cowboy." It was a girl whose hand he'd encountered. No, a woman. She was only the size of a girl. In fact, she was probably the little, bittiest damn grown woman he'd ever seen. The size of a ten- or eleven-year-old girl but definitely grown and probably much older than Dex was, as he could see from the lines and wrinkles at her eyes and throat. Eyes, hands and throat are always a giveaway.

Not that this girl—woman—was trying to hide anything.

Far from it. She was wearing a dress that exposed nearly all of her chest. She didn't have much there worth the bother of hiding anyway, as he could plainly see.

She wore enough powder to simulate a mask and had streaked both cheeks and her lips with a perfectly hideous shade of vermilion war paint.

Dex suspected that this woman was not a courthouse clerk here to enjoy a short one on her way home.

"You're handsome, cowboy," she ventured. Her voice was young even if the rest of her was not, and her smile seemed sincere.

Dex gave her high marks for that. A person who can do a good job of faking sincerity will always make out okay.

"You're also not a cowboy," she said. "We don't get many gents in here."

"It's the closest place to the livery," he said honestly. "Are there better places in town?"

"Not to my way of thinking," she said. "Maybe to yours. Me, I like it here just fine." She took a sliver of ham off the plate and popped it into her mouth, then took one pickled egg but instead of eating it at once dropped it into a pocket sewn onto the front of her dress.

Dex laughed.

"What's wrong?" she asked, uncertain where the humor came from.

"That egg. It makes you look, uh, lopsided."

The woman looked down at herself, then she laughed too. "I'd take another egg, but I don't have a pocket on that side." She settled for removing the egg and eating it.

"Want to fuck, cowboy?" she asked around a mouthful of crumbling egg bits.

"You're subtle," he said.

"Look, subtlety is for the young ones. Me, I grab for

what I can get. And I haven't been with a nice looking, clean fella like you in . . ." she grinned, "never you mind how long it's been."

"Got any diseases you know of?" he asked.

"Cowboy, I been in this racket long enough to know how to take care of myself. Take mighty good care of you too, believe me."

"How much for all night?" he asked, thinking about things like bedbugs in cheap hotel rooms and rats infesting livery barns.

"Two dollars," she told him. "And I'll give you all you can handle."

"You got bedbugs?"

"Naw. Their little thingies are too small to do me any good. But if you want some . . ." She grinned again.

Dex laughed. He found himself kind of liking the tiny, wee whore with the horrid makeup and a ready grin.

And two dollars beat hell out of five, especially with the extra services provided.

Much better than hot springs and a stupid mud bath, any day of the week.

"Okay, lady. You've got yourself a customer for the night." He drained away the last swallow of beer, helped himself to one of those eggs and motioned for the little woman to lead on.

• 15 •

"I'm Annabelle, cowboy. What would you like me to call you?"

"You can call me whatever you like, but my name is Dexter Lee Yancey."

"Honey, that sounds like your real name."

"And so it is, Annabelle."

"Now you've got me to feeling ashamed of myself, Dexter Lee Yancey. So whyn't you call me Amanda." She paused in the act of unlocking a crib door and rolled her eyes upward in deep thought for several seconds. "God, Dexter Lee, I bet it's been ten, fifteen years since I gave any man my real name."

"In that case, Amanda, I consider myself to be duly honored by your trust." He bowed to her.

The little whore managed to open the sticky lock and gave the door a push.

"After you," Dex said, motioning for her to go ahead.

She gave him a very strange look, then hurried in ahead of him and turned up the wick on a bedside lamp that had been left burning on a very low flame. Dex followed her inside and bolted the door closed behind them, locking the cares of the world outside at least for the time being.

Amanda's workplace was not exactly the lap of luxury. The clapboard walls were nothing more than bare framing with the wide, board sheathing nailed on the outside. No attempt had been made to finish the interior. Amanda or some previous occupant had pasted up several woodcut pictures—barnyard and woods scenes—that looked like they had been cut out of magazines.

The room, one of eight or ten in the row that stretched out behind the saloon, was perhaps six feet wide and twice that deep. A wooden shelf had been built across the back wall to fashion the bed. It held a thick mattress, sheets and pair of pillows. Underneath this permanently mounted bed were a pair of shoes and a small traveling case at one end and a heavy crockery thundermug at the other.

At the front of the room on the side opposite the doorway there was a sheet metal stove of the type known as a sheepherder's stove and beside that a rocking chair. An upended crate set beside the head of the bed served as a bedside table. It held the lamp on top and a basin and pitcher below.

Pegs on the wall were draped with a cape and bonnet, a dark dress—probably Amanda's go-to-town dress, for she damn sure couldn't appear on the public streets in her working clothes—and, close to the table, some towels. A rag rug had been laid beside the bed.

If the place was Spartan, and it was, it was also tidy. Dex had been in much finer places, of course. But then he'd also been in some worse too.

"Make yourself comfortable, Dexter Lee. And if it wouldn't offend you any, I'd kinda prefer it if you'd take your boots off. Not that you have to or anything. But it'd be nice."

"I have no intention of sleeping in my clothing," he allowed. "Could I ask a favor of you, Amanda?"

"Sure, honey. Anything. I told you that a'ready."

"Then would you please wash your face? I'm betting there's a real pretty girl underneath all that paint and plaster, and I'd like to see what she looks like."

"Dexter Lee, are you sure that . . ."

"Please," he repeated.

Her expression reflected some very obvious misgivings about this request. But she did as he asked and without further objection reached for the washbasin and water pitcher.

While Amanda was occupied with that, Dex laid two dollars in currency on the lamp table and stripped off his clothes.

• 16 •

Her pubic hair was salt-and-pepper gray—more salt than pepper, really—and he revised his guess at her age upward by a good ten years or so to a point that probably should have made him ashamed of himself to be bedding her.

Without the war paint Amanda was a rather drab little bit of a thing hardly larger than a breadbox and with no more meat on her than a coursing hound. She was all bone and sinew, and when he tried to put his hands around her waist he could actually, literally get his fingertips to touch while barely squeezing.

Her belly was as flat as his. And her chest was damn near as shapeless. Her tits consisted of dark, little nipples about the size of raisins set in the middle of small, very slightly rounded protrusions no larger than a demitasse saucer.

She'd colored her hair with henna or some similar product so that he had no idea what it would have looked like originally.

She was, he discovered to his great surprise, kind of shy once she took the makeup off. It occurred to him that the thick paint acted as a mask for her to hide behind, gave her a role she could play as if on a stage so that her real self would not be exposed to the ugliness of her trade. Now, without that deception to protect her, perhaps she was vulnerable and open to the hurt of insults and abuses that would otherwise be directed at the phony actress called Annabelle.

Dex sat on the side of the bed and opened his arms to her when she finished washing and, naked, turned to him.

She gave a nervous laugh and a toss of her head and said, "I can put it all back if you want, cowboy."

"Not a chance." He smiled. "I told you I thought I'd find a pretty girl under that goo. An' so I did. Come here, Amanda. Come here, pretty girl." Pretty was an exaggeration. But hell, it doesn't cost anything to be nice to someone. And he really did like her a whole lot better this way than before.

She came to him, unsure and holding herself stiffly, and he held her for a moment. He was seated and she was standing but even so her head barely topped his. He could feel her slim body relax after a few moments, and he looked up, cupping her chin in his hand.

Then, deliberately and slowly, he kissed her.

Amanda gasped and pulled away from him. But only by a fraction of an inch.

"Are you . . . are you sure you wanta do that, honey? Dexter Lee, I mean? Are you sure you want to kiss me, knowin' what it is that I do?"

By way of an answer he kissed her again, and Amanda melted into him. Her mouth opened to his, and he felt her tremble. He wondered how long it had been since this shy little bawd was kissed by anyone.

Dex picked her up—she weighed scarcely more than his saddle; hell, maybe less—and placed her gently down onto the bed at his side. He kissed her all the more then, long and slow, and gently toyed with her nipples while he did so.

When he reached down to finger her mound he was surprised to find that she was wet there, slippery with her own natural juices and in need of nothing more than that to ease his entry.

It would've been an insult to refuse such an invitation, he believed, and so without breaking their kiss he raised himself above her and pressed down.

His erection needed no guide. Amanda opened herself to him, and he slid easily into the warm, sweet depths of her body, her flesh surrounding his and molding itself to accommodate.

Funny, he thought, how the extreme difference in their heights made no difference now.

But then all women are the same height when they're lying down, he supposed. Just as all looked the same in the dark.

Amanda's arms crept around him and then her legs so that she clung to him with all the tenacity and subtle strength of an amorous leech, and when he began to rock back and forth on top of her her breath quickened and she began to moan softly in the rhythm of his slow and gentle thrusting.

Dex was in no hurry about this one. If anything, this first time was for Amanda. It would take the edge off his own needs.

And they had the whole night long in which to play and explore.

Now that he was here he was, he found, quite looking forward to it all.

Yessir, it was just one damn fine thing that he hadn't submitted to the larceny of that hotel with the mud baths because he would far rather bathe in this little woman's sweat and juices than in that place's hot springs.

Then the soft, slow pleasures began to gather and rise into more urgent ones, and he had neither time nor interest in thoughts beyond these marvelous immediate sensations.

• 17 •

Dex took Amanda to breakfast the next morning, out in public as if she were a lady. And indeed, save for the rather regrettable coloring of her hair she even looked the part of a respectable townswoman. Acted the role too with one exception.

"Would you do me a big favor, Dexter Lee?"

"Of course I will."

"I'd rather you call me Annabelle when we're out among regular folks if you don't mind. I kinda don't want anybody to know what my real name is." She smiled. "Except you, honey."

He'd been pleased to accommodate her—after all, she had certainly accommodated his every wish and whim the whole night through, and then some—and he thoroughly enjoyed the little woman's company through the meal.

Afterward he reclaimed his horse from the livery and was back in Winter Grove in time for a late lunch. First, though, he wanted to pay a visit to the town jail to assure himself that James was faring well despite the unpleasant circumstances of the moment.

"Afternoon, Marshal," Dex said when he got there. "You

don't look pleased to see me. You wouldn't want to hurt my feelings now, would you?"

"When I heard you'd left town, Mr. Yancey, I hoped you were taking my advice about going."

"Convention calls for me to tell you that I'm sorry to've disappointed you, Marshal, but you know better than that. I'm not sorry the least bit."

"Now that you've returned, Mr. Yancey, what can I do for you?"

"It looks like I'll be representing my friend's case before the court myself. I needed to consult with a colleague at the county seat, you understand, but now I look forward to being able to present my case before Judge . . . um . . . Gressley, was it?"

"Close," Harris said. "It's Grassley. Now what is this about you representing the defendant? You never mentioned yesterday that you're a lawyer."

"That is because I wanted to make sure my credentials before the Louisiana bar would be honored here, sir. I've been assured by the gentlemen in Connor that this will pose no problem." The only bar Dex ever stood before was the kind that served liquor and beer. But he considered that to be a mere technicality.

"That may well be, Mr. Yancey, but your point is moot."

"How is that, Marshal?"

"You are too late to make that appearance, sir. Judge Grassley heard the case this morning with Curtis Blake as complainant and your man representing himself."

"Dammit," Dex blurted.

Harris shrugged. "It was like I told you, Mr. Yancey. The sentence is for five months. He could earn five days off that if he works good and gives me no trouble. And I meant what I said yesterday. He'll be treated pretty much the same as a white man. Fed good, not worked more than a strong back can handle. You can tell him where it is you want to meet him when his sentence is done, and I'll get him there for you."

"What about my money belt? You have it locked up someplace in your office here."

"I won't try and make this any tougher than it has to be, Mr. Yancey. Wait one second there. I'll give you the money belt. You'll have to sign for it, of course, and your nigger will have to sign off on it too."

"All right." Dex glanced toward the back of the small jail where James was lying on one of the steel bunks with the blanket wadded under his ear like a pillow and his back to the room. He looked like he was sleeping, but Dex didn't believe that for a minute.

"Can I tell him that?" Dex asked.

"You go right ahead."

Dex took a pencil and the inventory sheet Harris handed him and carried them to the cell door.

"Not too close, please. I'll want to be seeing everything that passes between your hands there."

"Of course, Marshal."

James gave up his pretense and came to the front of the cell to accept the form and sign it.

"You doing all right?" Dex whispered.

"Just fucking wonderful," James growled back. He sounded bitter. Not that Dex blamed him.

"I'll find a way to get you out," Dex said. "That's a promise."

"Well don't try to break me out. This place is built solid. Believe me; I've looked it over. Had nothing better to do."

"I said I'd find a way, James. I will."

"I know, I . . . it isn't you I'm pissed at, Dex."

"I know that."

"Isn't Marshal Harris either, come to that. He's doing like he said. He's treating me decent. For a damned prisoner."

"Sure."

"Dex."

"Yeah, buddy?"

"Make this quick as you can, will you?"

"I will, James. Count on it." Dex glanced down at the inventory sheet. James had signed. The signature read: James Yancey in the clear and fluid script they'd both been taught.

Dex wondered if . . . no, this wasn't the time to bring that up. Later. When James was free to walk the streets again. They could talk about such things then.

"That's long enough," Harris said. "Visiting hours aren't until after supper. And I'm hoping you won't still be in town, Mr. Yancey. Remember what I've told you. It is still excellent advice."

Dex nodded a silent good-bye to James, then took the signed form back to the marshal and exchanged it for the money belt.

Dex had no idea where he should go from here, but there was at least the possibility that he would be needing a war chest to finance his campaign to free James.

And while he did not know where that effort would ultimately lead, he did know where he intended to go for the next step along that path.

· 18 ·

"Mr. Yancey. It's a pleasure to see you again." She smiled. "And during business hours this time, I notice. Well, I did make the offer. Feel free to choose any of my girls. There will be no charge."

Dex swept his hat off and bowed low. "As I believe I mentioned earlier, dear lady, that is an offer I would only wish to accept if you yourself were my . . . hostess and counselor. No other could compare, none other satisfy I am sure."

"You flatter me, sir." But the smile returned and with even more intensity. "Besides, you haven't seen my girls."

"I don't need to see them, Mrs. Adams. I've seen you."

"Goodness, I haven't been so complimented since I was a debutante."

"Then the gentlemen here are lacking in either their eyesight or their judgment."

She laughed, obviously enjoying his attentions. "The sad truth, Mr. Yancey, is that there are no gentlemen here. Or there were none until you arrived."

"Then I pity them their deficiencies, m'lady."

"Oh, I do wish I'd known you when I was a girl, Mr. Yancey. I would have fluttered my lashes most outrageously, but I think my heart would have palpitated even faster." She laughed again.

"May I ask where you were in those innocent times, Mrs. Adams?"

"In Mississippi, sir."

"Had I only known I would have thrown myself into the great river and swum across if no other means presented itself. There was not a belle in all of Louisiana who could have compared."

"Please. I've forgotten my manners to've kept you standing in the vestibule like this. May I show you to the parlor? You really should see my ladies. One look could cause you to change your mind."

"Never," he said stoutly. "But I would like to come in. Would it be inconvenient for us to speak in your office again? I know you are busy now, so if this is not a good time . . ."

"I am in your debt, Mr. Yancey. I will always find time for you. Besides, it is still early. We'll not be busy until past nine."

Dex surrendered his hat and cane to the black maid, Betty Lou, and followed Eleanor Adams back into the office.

On his way past the wide-open double doors he did get a glimpse of the parlor. Eleanor Adams was right about one thing. She had very good-looking girls working for her. At least the two Dex saw were very pretty. Therefore probably expensive as well. Neither looked to've left her teens yet, and both were dressed in entirely ladylike gowns, with no gaudy makeup or improbable hair colorings. Dex couldn't help but think of little Amanda/Annabelle back in Connor. But then Amanda was sweet and great good fun to be with. There was something to be said for that too.

Not that his attention belonged on the ladies of the evening. Not right now. He had other fish to fry.

"Tea, Betty Lou, for both of us. Mr. Yancey takes his with lemon and two sugars." Now how the hell had she remembered a piddling little thing like that, he wondered.

"Yessum." The maid closed the door on her way out.

"You've been to the county seat," she said. It was not a question. "Did you learn anything there?"

"D'you keep track of everything that goes on around here?"

"Pretty much so. At least the things and the people that interest me. My girls have big ears, you see."

"And now it's my turn to feel flattered. I'm glad I interest you."

The woman blushed. Incredible, Dex thought. Here she was, the madam of a luxurious and obviously successful whorehouse, and she sat right there and blushed a vivid shade of red that did nothing to compliment the rich auburn of her hair. "That is *not* what I said, Mr. Yancey."

"No, it was not. Forgive me, please." Not that he meant it. Nor would she likely think that he did.

"You were about to say?" she asked.

"Yes, sorry." He filled her in on the little he'd learned in Connor. While he was talking the maid came in with their tea. It was already prepared exactly the way he liked it. His gratitude, of course, was expressed to Mrs. Adams and not directly to the servant. Betty Lou bowed her way quietly out of the room again, and Dex returned to the subject at hand. "My visit to the courthouse turned out very much like you told me to expect."

She nodded. "So where do you go from here? Will you accept the marshal's advice?"

He had no intention of commenting on how in hell she would already know what Marshal Harris advised. It was enough to be aware that she did.

"Not until James is out of that jail," he said.

"This nigra of yours. He is . . . I mean he was your slave?"

Dex nodded. It would not be prudent to offer explanations to a well-bred girl from Mississippi. "He was my play-boy from the time we were both babies."

"Yes, of course." She looked wistful. Nostalgic for the old days, Dex supposed, back when a woman like her would have owned colored servants like Betty Lou. Or James.

"Anyway," he said, wanting to get back to the purpose for his visit this evening, "I need to arrange a change of venue. And for that I need Judge Grassley's cooperation."

"But you couldn't find a lawyer in Connor who would help you. Isn't that what you said?"

"Yes." He grinned. "So I expect I'll just have to serve as James's legal counsel myself."

"But you're not a lawyer."

"Of course I am," Dex protested.

"Mr. Yancey. Really! A gentleman of your breeding . . . kin to the Lees and the Custises . . . would never consent to becoming anything so disreputable as a lawyer. A scholar perhaps. A planter certainly. A dilettante and gambler. Even a drunkard and thief. But a lawyer? Never."

Dex's grin returned. "I know that," he said. "You know that. But your Judge Grassley won't know that. And if I say that I'm a member of the bar back home . . ." He spread his hands and shrugged. "What I want you to do, Mrs. Adams, is have your girls spread a few lies on my behalf. Information can travel in two directions, don't you see. And I don't need to win my case here. All I need to do is muddy the water enough to convince Judge Grassley that it would be in his best interest to reopen the case against James and have it transferred to Connor. Let him wash his hands of it, so to speak."

"I'm sorry, Mr. Yancey. Really I am. But your plan couldn't possibly work."

"Why not? I can throw enough bullfeathers into the air to keep the town butcher from seeing clearly. I promise you that."

"It isn't Herb Grassley that I'm thinking of, Mr. Yancey. It's Curtis Blake. He would never fall for it."

"But . . ."

"Mr. Yancey. Believe me. Curtis is from the South himself. He's from east Texas. And I happen to know that he has practiced in Louisiana himself in the past. He used to have a practice in Shreveport. I've heard him talk about it. You couldn't possibly fool him into believing you. And he would certainly know that a Lee or a Yancey wouldn't consider the law as a profession. Not short of an elected position as judge. Not a man like you." She shook her head. "Perhaps you don't realize it, Mr. Yancey, but anyone who knows the South and knows gentlemanly breeding and demeanor can take one look at you and see you for who you are. I can and Curtis Blake can too. And I can tell you something else, Mr. Yancey. Curtis Blake is jealous of you. He resents your background. He probably very much resents you still having a nigra after all these years when he himself never did have one. No, Mr. Yancey, Curtis would never let you get away with your plan. And without Curtis's consent, Herb Grassley would never allow reconsideration of the case against your man."

She looked genuinely sorrowful when she told him, "I would help you in any way I can, Mr. Yancey. Indeed I shall if you can think of something workable. But the truth is that the only way Herb would ever allow your man relief from his sentence would be if Curtis Blake asked him to."

Dex smiled. "Why, in that case, Mrs. Adams, it appears that I'll have to get Mr. Blake to drop his charges against James and have the judge reconsider the conviction."

• 19 •

"And just how, may I ask, will you go about having Curtis change his mind?"

Dex shrugged and grinned. "Darned if I know exactly how. Yet. But I'll think of something. Kinda slip up unnoticed like a snake in tall grass and strike when he's not expecting it." He laughed as if to imply that he didn't really mean that. But in fact he did. C. Julian Blake was *not* going to be allowed to do this to James.

"I certainly wish you luck, I . . ."

Whatever she intended to say remained unspoken as Betty Lou came bustling into the office without knocking or waiting to be invited. "Miz Adams, ma'am. You best come."

"Excuse me." Eleanor Adams hurried away in an explosion of swirling crinolines and Dex, with absolutely nothing else to do, stood and idled along in her wake.

"I already told you, you little nigger bitch, go upstairs and get Marguerite. And Elizabeth too while you're at it. Now do it. Quick before I take a whip to your black ass."

It was C. Julian Blake who was loudly blustering in the whorehouse foyer. Dex might have understood—a little—

if the SOB was drunk, but he appeared to be cold sober. Just bone-deep mean. But sober.

"Curtis. Calm down. I know you like Marguerite, and I will be happy to send her to you just as soon as she is available. But she is with a gentleman already, and it wouldn't be right . . ."

"Damn what's right. I want Marguerite and I want her right now or I'll thrash your nigger here and you too. D'you hear me? Now tell this stupid cunt to call Marguerite out. And Elizabeth. I want both of them tonight. D'you hear?"

"Curtis, I cannot possibly . . ."

Blake punched her.

The son of a bitch didn't slap her or clip her lightly. He balled his fist and struck Eleanor Adams flush in the face.

He acted as if he fully intended to do it again, but he didn't have time for that.

Standing at the door to the piano room, Dex was too far away to stop Blake from hitting the woman the first time. But for the second time in as many days he was there to block Blake's arm and intercept the following attempt.

And this time he did not intend to allow Curtis Blake any opportunity to backshoot him.

This time Dexter Yancey's firm intention was to beat the crap out of the Winter Grove lawyer.

Dex grabbed Blake's forearm in his left hand and hauled down on it, keeping the second punch from reaching Eleanor. He gave Blake no time to react. Dex stepped forward and turned partially away as if to present his back to the lawyer. Far from that, he drove the point of his right elbow as hard as he could into the bigger man's solar plexus, emptying his lungs of air and turning Blake pale as the linen wrappings that held his broken jaw in place.

The big man likely would have gulped for air if he'd been able, but the constriction of the wrapping kept him from opening his mouth more than a fraction of an inch.

While Blake was occupied with his immediate need for breath, Dex took half a step backward and weighed his choices.

Fairness demanded that he pause and give Blake a

chance to recover. Decency and honorable conduct would require that he take pains—literally if necessary—to avoid making worse an injury previously sustained.

But then decent and honorable men do not go around beating on women who are not their wives. Not even if the woman happened to operate a whorehouse.

No, Dex concluded, C. Julian Blake was himself not a man given to decency and honor.

Besides, dammit, Dex didn't like him.

So . . . fuck the lawyer.

Dex waited until Blake lifted his chin in an effort to draw more air in past barely parted lips.

And then, with deliberation and malice aforethought, Dex planted his best right-hand smack onto the linen padded shelf of Curtis Blake's broken jaw.

Blake didn't scream or for that matter make much of any sound beyond a high, thin keening.

The big son of bitch's eyes rolled back in his head, and he passed out cold.

"I think," Dex said, "you'd best have somebody carry him to your town doctor."

◆ 20 ◆

"Please. You should get away from here. Please listen to me," Eleanor Adams pleaded for the third or fourth time. They were again in her office. Dex assumed by then someone would have carted C. Julian Blake away for necessary repairs. Assumed that, but didn't know it. And furthermore didn't much care. Miserable SOB.

"I'm not afraid of him," Dex said. Modesty prevented him from pointing out that he'd already whipped the big asshole twice. Well, modesty plus the fact that Mrs. Adams already knew it. Dex knew better than to belabor a point already made.

"You don't understand," the woman said. "Curtis is not . . . a nice man."

Dex couldn't help but smile at that. "Let's see now. Twice in two days he's tried to rough you up. Tried to shoot me in the back. What else?" He shrugged. "And now you're wondering if I've yet figured out that he is not a 'nice man'? Mrs. Adams, I can assure you that the possibility already crossed my mind."

"That isn't what I meant. It's that . . . you shouldn't trust Curtis. I mean you *really* shouldn't trust him. He might . . . God knows what means he may resort to next. He obviously can't face you himself. I wouldn't put it at all past him to hire someone to do that for him now that you've finished the job you started on his jaw yesterday."

"I can't leave without James. And I can't get him out of jail until your friend Blake tells the judge to let him out."

"Well I don't think you can count on Curtis doing you any favors," she said, the understatement bringing another smile to Dex's face. "Besides, you could leave if you wanted to. Surely your friend would understand. I could explain it to him if you like. I could tell him what a truly mean and despicable man Curtis is. Your problem, Mr. Yancey, is not that you can't go but that you won't."

"Okay," he admitted without rancor. "I could go but I won't. Does that make you feel better?"

"It makes me feel simply terrible. It means you will probably wind up dead, just like . . ."

Dex waited, but she did not go on.

"Just like who?" he asked.

She shook her head. "Never mind. I don't know anything. Not for sure, I mean. But please believe me. Curtis Blake is a very dangerous man."

"So am I," Dex said softly. "Could I ask you a highly rude and personal question, Mrs. Adams?"

"You can ask me anything, Mr. Yancey. My debt to you has been doubled. There is very little that I could deny you, sir."

"This is probably none of my business, but it's pretty obvious that you are very much at odds with Blake too. After all, it's you he has been threatening and trying to strike. If it isn't too personal a question, may I ask . . . why?"

She spun her chair away and seemed lost in thought for several moments. "Would you care for some brandy?" she asked when she turned back to face him again.

Dex suspected she was buying time for more thought. "Yes I would, thank you."

Eleanor rose gracefully and went to a sideboard where she produced a cut crystal decanter and a pair of balloon snifters. Dex noticed that her hand was shaking when she poured the amber liquid. Her face did not betray the nervousness, but her hands certainly did.

"This is excellent," he said after she'd served him and he had a chance to taste the brandy. Eleanor did not appear to hear. She returned to her chair and again sat for several minutes in silence.

Finally she looked up. "I . . . work for Curtis Blake. He really owns the business here. He thinks . . . he seems to think that this means he owns me too."

"I see," Dex said, although he realized full well that he probably didn't see at all. Certainly not the entire situation. "Tell me about it, please."

Once Eleanor started it came pouring out in a rush. Dex suspected it was a story she'd never told nor so much as hinted at before. Not to anyone. Now that the words were coming it was as if she couldn't wait to get them all out, and probably it was easier for her knowing that he was a stranger and not likely to have anyone in or near Winter Grove with whom to share gossip.

• 21 •

"I have made many mistakes, Mr. Yancey, and one of the biggest of them was when I married Ned Adams. My maiden name was . . . let me just say it is a name you probably would recognize."

He nodded.

"Our family lost everything during the war. Everything except our name and our honor. I am sure you've heard the same from all too many fine old Southern families."

"Unfortunately I have, yes."

"I was just fifteen when my mother died and sixteen when my father took his own life in his grief and pain. I was left with nothing. Then I read an advertisement about the wonderful opportunities to be found in the western lands. And about the lack of ladies for the gentlemen to marry. The article mentioned a service. A . . . matrimonial service. Gentlemen paid a fee in order to meet . . . by mail, that is . . . and correspond with young ladies who might be willing to become their wives. The service was free for the ladies. It only cost me the three cents' postage to register my name with the agency." Her expression became bitter. "Three cents and all my hope for happiness. That is what it cost me." She paused and took a sip of the brandy.

"I received many letters, most from men who were ten, twenty, even thirty years older than I. Ned Adams was thirty-four years my elder." Her chin lifted a fraction of an inch, a defiant little go-to-hell gesture. "I chose him, Mr. Yancey, because unlike the others he had land holdings. The others were clerks, miners, one a trail boss, whatever that might be. Ned had land, and it was land that was once the basis for my family's prosperity. When the land was lost, so was the prosperity. I wanted to have land again, and Ned promised he would put the land deed in my name immediately upon our marriage. He had," she laughed, "can you believe it, Mr. Yancey? Esau sold his hope of the future for a bowl of stew. I sold mine for three hundred twenty acres. Half a section. Can you believe that?" She looked like she was about to cry.

Dex grunted softly, trying to make the sound a sympathetic one. He took another sip of his brandy.

"Silly me. Silly, silly, stupid me." She shook her head. "I knew, of course, that three hundred twenty acres is not enough to make a man really wealthy. But a half section of Mississippi black soil will make a man very comfortable. A man and his family. I had no idea that not all land is so . . . productive. Here . . . three hundred twenty acres of baked dirt and brown weeds won't keep two cows and a mule unless there is live water on the place. And there was none on Ned's half section. He and his late wife each filed on a quarter section, and they were unlucky enough to have rain until they were able to prove up and gain title. I say they were unlucky about that because if they'd failed they would have moved on, perhaps even prospered somewhere else. Who knows what might have been different had they claimed land somewhere else." She stopped and turned her chair to stare into some unseen and unseeable distance again for a bit.

"Sorry," she said after a moment. But she continued to face away from him when she resumed her tale. "Ned was as good as his word. We met at the railroad station in Denver and were married there. Then he brought me home."

The bitterness in her voice was even thicker when she repeated "home" as if it were a cussword.

"Home, you see, was a one-room sod house out there
near the holes where he'd tried to make a well but failed.
Three times he'd failed to find water. We had to get it in
town and carry it out. Ned hadn't told me any of that. Nor
that the rains failed too. He hardly got more corn than he'd
planted seed. He failed at that just like the rest, and I suppose he would have failed off the farm too if he'd lived
long enough. Instead that sad, sorry old failure even failed
at failing. He died and left me a young widow with three
hundred twenty acres of useless land and a large debt that
Ned incurred over several years. He'd borrowed money for
the seed, you see, so he could plant more corn that wouldn't
grow. And so he could send the train ticket so I could come
out here to marry him and be his house servant."

Dex wasn't sure Eleanor had even noticed it, but there
were tears streaming from her eyes and making silvery,
shining runnels in the light powder that dusted her cheeks.

"Damn him," she said softly as she wept.

Dex pretended that he saw no tears, nor did she acknowledge them. He suspected she wanted to believe she was too
proud to cry. And too tough. "I gather," he said, "that the
note was held by Lawyer Blake?"

"Oh, you gather correctly about that, sir. But then he
made me a proposition. Not the one I might have expected
from him but almost as bad. I would front for him as pro-
prietor of this . . . establishment. He would provide everything else. I would be allowed to keep my land . . . not that
I wanted it by then, but I knew there would be no takers
for a useless half section even if I did try to sell . . . and
Curtis would have his whorehouse. His own playhouse it
is really. But I think the main reason he likes it is because
he can pump the girls for more than just sex. He uses them
for sex, of course. He's very rough. Sometimes it takes
them days to recover. But that isn't the only reason he
wanted this place. He also uses them to get information.
God knows what he does with the dirty little secrets he has
to hold over the men around here. Personally I don't even

want to know. I just wish . . ." She didn't bother to finish the sentence.

After a brief pause she said, "Curtis provides for my food and clothing. When there were documents that had to be signed and, once, a fine that had to be paid, he told me what to do and I did it. I have . . . no place else to go. No money. He still holds those notes over my head, so if I tried to leave he would just have Judge Grassley issue a warrant for my arrest. He has been threatening me with that. At this point I have . . . no hope left. No hope."

The tears continued to flow but, oddly Dex thought, she did not sob. Her shoulders never quivered. As far as he could tell even her breathing did not quicken. She simply sat there and tried to ignore the salty streams that trickled down her throat to disappear inside the neck of her gown.

Not a nice man, she'd said earlier about C. Julian Blake.

That seemed to be accurate enough.

Something occurred to Dex, a detail that she'd left out of her litany of pain, and he asked, "Why is he so angry with you now? It sounds like you've done everything the man wanted when he asked for this arrangement."

Eleanor gave him a haunted look and said, "I told you he didn't ask for the one thing that could have been worse. Well now he's demanding that too. He wants me to join him upstairs along with some of the other girls. Now he wants me to 'entertain' him too."

"I see," Dex said softly. And indeed he did.

He'd always thought it damned stupid for a woman to claim there could be a "fate worse than death."

Now, with Curtis Blake in mind, he wasn't so sure about that.

· 22 ·

The night deputy jumped to his feet when Dex walked into the jail, stopping by to visit with James before he went back to the hotel. "The marshal's wantin' to see you, mister."

Fine. I'll stop by sometime tomorrow during his hours."

"No, I mean he's wantin' to see you right away."

"All right, I'll visit with my friend while you go tell him that I'm here."

The deputy shook his head. "I can't be leavin' you alone with the prisoner. You might sneak him contraband or somethin'." The fellow stumbled a little over the word 'contraband'. Dex wondered if he knew what it meant. Or if he thought it was something that came in packets. Contraband. Highest quality. Ace Brand. Never a dissatisfied customer. Always choose Ace for your Contraband.

"What would you suggest, Deputy . . . uh . . . I'm sorry, I've forgotten your name."

"Names's Tyler. Deputy Marshal Emmett Tyler. And I can't let you alone with the prisoner. Marshal's rules."

"We certainly wouldn't want to violate any of the marshal's rules." Dex smiled. "Contraband and all that."

"Right," Tyler agreed solemnly. "Tell you what, mister.

Whyn't you see the marshal first thing. I'll let you see the prisoner when you get back."

"All right."

"I don't think he's to home yet though. Try at the doc's office first. He's likely still there."

"And that would be . . . ?"

Tyler gave him directions—Winter Grove wasn't so awfully big that it was hard to get around—and Dex ambled over there, his stomach rumbling just a bit to remind him that it was past the dinner hour and he hadn't yet taken time to have his supper.

The doctor's office was on the second floor of the bank building. A very handsome, professionally cast brass sign announced the premises as belonging to Gordon Stuart, M.D., D.D.S., Ph.D. Obviously a man of many parts this Doc Stuart of theirs. Dex had to wonder why a man with such credentials would be languishing in a backwater like Winter Grove when he could have been practicing his trade—or trades—in a more lucrative clime.

Dex mounted the exterior staircase and tapped lightly on the door there. He could see lights and movement through the frosted glass so he was sure the office was still open.

"Yes?" The door was opened to him by a very thin and pale young man who wore a pencil mustache and oiled curls in his hair. There was something decidedly off-putting about the man, but Dex couldn't quite decide just why that was so. "May I help you?"

Ah, that was it. The slightly fey appearance. The hint of lisp in the speech. No woman would ever need fear this one. Small boys, on the other hand should probably be wary.

"You're Doc Stuart?"

"I am the doctor's nurse, sir. How may I help you?"

Which, Dex thought, explained why a man with three degrees listed behind his name would be in a village like this rather than in Denver or Kansas City or even New Orleans.

"I'm looking for the marshal."

"Of course, sir. Will you come inside?"

Dex accepted the invitation and made himself comfortable in a maplewood armchair while the nurse minced delicately away into the back of the place. The doctor apparently had the whole second floor. Perhaps Stuart and his nurse lived here too.

Tom Harris came out in a minute or so and settled heavily into the chair next to Dex's. "I am not pleased to see you again so soon, Mr. Yancey."

"If you'll recall, sir, it wasn't my idea."

"Curtis's jaw seems to've been damaged again. Would you know anything about that?"

"What does he say?" Dex countered.

"Say? Curtis can't 'say' anything. Doc has had to reset the jaw—which he tells me is a very tricky proposition that may or may not work—and this time he's fashioned an iron brace that Curtis will have to wear for at least six weeks. God knows if he will ever get full mobility again."

"You mean he may mumble from now on? Goodness. That'd be terrible for a lawyer, wouldn't it."

"Don't make light of this, Mr. Yancey."

"Sorry."

"I do not believe that for a moment."

Dex shrugged.

"And I think you are most probably the person who inflicted this damage."

"You are entitled to your beliefs and opinions, Marshal."

"Are you denying that you hit Curtis Blake in the jaw, Mr. Yancey?"

"Marshal, I admitted to you already yesterday that I'm the one who broke his jaw. But to be accurate about this, I didn't hit him. I kicked the son of a bitch. Right after he tried to shoot me in the back."

"I already know that. I mean again. Today. Did you break his jaw again, Mr. Yancey?"

"Is it possible to break something that's already broken? Now there is an interesting point, don't you think?"

"You have not answered my question."

"All right then. For the record, Marshal, I neither admit nor deny. Which is, I believe, my right."

"In other words, you did it. I know you did it. I can't prove you did it," Harris said.

"Do you have an accusation, Marshal? The, uh, victim might not be able to speak, but I'd think he could write out a note if he wanted to charge somebody with a crime."

"Curtis hasn't seen fit to do that. He hasn't told me anything at all. Before Doc Stuart knocked him out with the ether so he could work on the jaw without Curtis screaming and thrashing about, Curtis wrote only one note. That was an instruction that his, um, employee Joshua Bonner be brought to him. Bonner is in there now waiting for his boss to wake up."

"I'm sure he has his reasons, Marshal."

"Dammit, Mr. Yancey, I am trying to do you a favor here. You don't know Josh Bonner."

"Nossir, I don't believe I've had the pleasure."

"You won't find it any pleasure if . . . I would advise you, Mr. Yancey, to leave Winter Grove. Immediately. Before Curtis wakes up from that ether."

"Just what sort of work does this Bonner do for Blake, Marshal?"

"Nothing illegal that I know about, I can assure you, or he would have been behind bars a long time ago. But . . ." The marshal groped for the words he wanted. "My advice to you is heartfelt, Mr. Yancey. I do not like trouble in my town. I do not want any harm to come to you or to anyone else."

"You wouldn't want to be more specific about your warning would you, Marshal?"

That wasn't fair and Dex knew it. He was taunting the straight-arrow town marshal, knowing the man was genuinely concerned with keeping the peace but could not make accusations about things that he only believed to be true without knowing absolutely that they were.

This line of conversation, though, was making him more than a little curious about Joshua Bonner and the duties he might perform on Curtis Blake's behalf.

The marshal could only give Dex a bleak look and a shake of the head.

"I want to get my friend out of your jail, Marshal. He wouldn't ride off and leave me if I were the one sitting behind those bars."

"Would it be worth suffering grave injuries, Mr. Yancey?"

"Grave injuries," Dex repeated thoughtfully. "Like, oh, a badly broken jaw? Something like that?"

"Or worse," Harris said. "It could even be worse."

"Much worse?"

The marshal's mouth opened. But no words came out. He wanted to say something. Dex was sure of it. But he couldn't. Fairness, law or simply the fact that he could prove none of his suspicions kept him from saying anything more about the extent of the consequences if Curtis Blake decided to become a law of his own . . . as Dex now was sure Tom Harris believed the man had done at least once before now.

"Never mind," Dex said. "I gather you're not charging me with any crime, Marshal?"

"I almost wish I could, Mr. Yancey. Not that I have anything against you, but I know you aren't likely to take my advice. It's just that I know you would be safe in my jail, you and your friend both."

"Thank you for the warning, Marshal." Dex stood. "If there is nothing else . . . ?"

"No. No charges. Nothing else."

"In that case, sir, I think I'll go visit with James for a little while, then see if I can't find a bite of supper."

"Good night, Mr. Yancey."

"Good night, sir."

• 23 •

Dex checked the time courtesy of a wall clock in the hotel lobby. Half past eleven in the morning. Definitely too early to go pounding on the whorehouse door. No one would likely be awake there for some hours. He wanted to speak with Eleanor Adams again to find out what she might know about this Bonner fellow that the marshal had warned him about.

If anyone in town had an inside line on Curtis Blake's employee it would be Eleanor and her girls.

Blake liked to use the "ladies of the night" to do his dirty digging? Dex thought it would be entirely appropriate to turn that same instrument against him. Bastard!

Too early for that now though.

Dex had had a restless sleep, then slept late once he did fall off. He'd had a late breakfast and probably wouldn't want to bother with lunch at all because of that. He couldn't pass the time visiting with James because they wouldn't allow that until evening.

He fingered his chin and decided that a shave would be in order. That would kill a little time. And maybe a trim and some bay rum scent too. Why not? Once the whore-house was open . . . surely it would be possible to sweet-talk Madame Adams into abandoning her principles long enough to entertain just one measly client.

And if not that, well, a man has needs. And that nice little Amanda over in the county seat seemed a long time in the past.

Dex stifled a yawn, his teeth chattering a little as he strove to keep his jaw shut, then ambled outside.

He was sure he'd seen a barber's pole on one of the side streets here. Now if he could only remember which one . . .

"Have a seat, mister. I won't be long."

Dex wasn't sure that was accurate. There was one man in the barber's chair already, and two more were waiting. Still, he hadn't anything better to do at the moment. If he had to wait anyway he could do it as easily here as anywhere.

He chose a seat that allowed him to keep an eye on the door. Not that he was worried by the marshal's warnings. Of course not. But a little caution never hurt.

There was damn-all little to read while he waited so he picked up the rumpled and often folded sheets of a newspaper from—he had to look at the masthead twice—Birmingham. Not the Birmingham he was familiar with though. And not the English city of that name either. This one was in New York State.

Birmingham, New York. He supposed he'd heard of it before. But he certainly never had any reason to pay attention to it. Nor to any other city, town or village in that far-off and decidedly foreign territory. Southern gentlemen had scant regard for any part of the North and for New York least of all. Well, that and Massachusetts maybe. Crazy sons of bitches in those places, all of them. Or so Dexter Lee Yancey and all his kin and neighbors were taught their whole lives long. Crazy as loons the whole pack of them and mean too. It was their greed that was responsible for the War and their cruelty that made the Reconstruction period so vile. Damn them. Damn them every one.

Dex felt no better for thinking about that, but having pondered it for a moment he went ahead and opened the

newspaper anyway. It was, after all, the only thing available
to read right now.

Crazy? Right there on the pages of that Birmingham
newspaper was proof positive that they were.

It seemed that for some years the people of New York
were bamboozled by the "discovery" and display of a fossilized giant. Except the giant was purely a fake, carved out
of gypsum and buried on a farm near some country hamlet
called Cardiff.

Apparently people paid good money to view the so-
called remains.

But that wasn't the part that Dex found so completely
amazing. The hoax was uncovered and the truth revealed
years ago. And *still* people were paying to see it.

The silly Yankee bastards paid to see the thing even
knowing it was a fake.

Or anywhere they still were as of—he had to turn back
to the masthead again for the date—as of nineteen months
past.

The story in this Birmingham paper gave the whole history of the thing, phoniness and all, and announced that a
traveling display would make the Cardiff Giant available
for viewing at the very reasonable price of ten cents.

Incredible! Ten cents. To look at a carved chunk of gypsum.

It was amazing what people could be talked into. Simply
amazing.

He smiled a little to himself, then turned the page and
went on perusing the old newspaper while one customer
left the barber's chair and another took his place.

One left to go and it would be Dex's turn. Better read a
little slower, he thought, and more thoroughly.

• 24 •

It wasn't that Eleanor Adams's whorehouse was so very far away. For it wasn't. And it wasn't that Dex was feeling lazy. Certainly not. But a horse needs exercise too. Of course it does. And it had been days now since James's animal was under saddle. The kind and sensible thing, therefore, would be for Dex to ride out to the whorehouse rather than walking the distance.

It was still fairly early but he could go for a canter out onto the prairie, then come back by way of the whorehouse.

He headed not for the outskirts of town but toward the livery stable where his horse and James's were eating hay at the rate of twenty-five cents per day. Each. Dex thought the amount a little high considering there was no grain included in the price.

He thought even more strongly that the cost was exorbitant when he got there and discovered there was no attendant on the premises. He would have to tack the animal himself, dammit, which probably meant that he would get his hands soiled. Or worse. And he'd dressed rather carefully in view of the meeting he planned with Eleanor Adams.

Still, there was nothing to be done about it now short of

walking out to the Adams place and risking becoming
sweaty. That would be worse than a little grime on the
palms.

He fetched his own plantation-style saddle out of the tack
room—it was much more comfortable than James's army
surplus McClellan would have been, and if the horse was
not familiar with it that was the horse's worry not his—
and James's bit and bridle. He draped them over the top
board of the indoor stall where the tall brown was standing,
propped his cane beside the gate and let himself in.

The horse snorted and eyed him a little warily but did
not lay its ears back or turn its butt ready to kick. Dex was
a familiar figure to the gelding even if not intimately so.

"Easy, boy. You doin' all right here?"

In the next stall over, Dex's horse whickered softly at
the sound of his voice.

Dex stroked the brown's neck and spent a few moments
scratching it in the hollow beneath the jaw, a spot horses
cannot reach by themselves and one that most delight in
having rubbed for them.

"You like that, boy? Do you?" Dex's voice was soft and
soothing.

"Hey, mister. You gonna kiss that sonuvabitch now?"

"Know what I think, Luis? The way he's sweet-talking
the bitch I think he's gonna fuck it. Kiss it first then run
around behind and fuck it. What you wanta bet he's got a
stool in there with him so's he can get hisself tall enough
to poke it in the ass."

"Is that right, mister? Is that horse stump broke so's you
can fuck it?"

Dex sent a none-too-appreciative glance toward the two
men who'd come into the barn. He did not recognize either
of them. Certainly neither was the liveryman he'd spoken
with when he brought the horses in to be quartered and
cared for.

One was a tall, lean Anglo with a tobacco-stained mustache and serious need of a shave. The other was shorter,
with dark features and a clean-cut look about him. That
was the one the other referred to as Luis. The Anglo looked

something of a simpleton. Luis most assuredly did not. He was compact, lithe and quite probably very quick.

The really disturbing thing, though, was that the Anglo had his belt gun in his hand and pointing in the general direction of Dex's belly.

The odds of a bullet fired from outside the stall traveling between the wooden rails were—what—fifty-fifty? Worse than that, however, was the thought that a bullet mutilated and sent tumbling by passing through the inch or so of wood would do even more damage to flesh than a normal slug.

Either way, through a rail or between them, Dex decided he really would rather not be shot this afternoon, thank you.

"Hey, mister. You wanta play?" Luis asked.

"Play?"

"I like to play this game sometimes. You know?"

"What game?"

"You Yankees, you call it tic and tac and toe, yes?"

"I've heard of the game. But don't call me a damn yankee. That could make me mad."

"You not no Yankee, mister?"

"No, I'm not. And the proper term is damnyankee. One word, not two."

"I kinda like you, mister. So I let you play the game with me." Luis reached into the small of his back and produced a slim, quite wicked-looking stiletto. From the way Luis held his weapon of choice Dex didn't have to test the edge with his thumb to know the knife was sharp. The blade looked to be a good seven or eight inches in length. Luis held it balanced delicately in his palm, not gripped in his fist. This boy was no amateur.

"We play the game on your stomach, okay?"

"I think not," Dex said.

"Oh, but I think we do. First one thing though, eh? First you take off the gunbelt there an' you hang it on the rail over there."

"I'm watchin' you, mister, an' believe me I won't miss if you try something," the Anglo warned.

Dex believed him.

"One thing more, yes? The other pistol you wear at your back? Put that onto the rail too, please."

Now how the hell would they have . . . oh. Of course. Dammit. He hadn't thought of that at the time, but he'd taken his coat off at the barber shop. He was sure neither of these men was in the place at the time, but someone had noticed his second Webley and obviously blabbed about it.

Lousy luck, that.

The Anglo raised his revolver a little and thumbed the hammer back ready to fire. The gesture wasn't strictly necessary. Any man who is reasonably capable with a firearm can cock and shoot with great speed. But as a threat and a warning, the sight and sound of a large-bore revolver being cocked is undeniably effective. The fact conveys a certain . . . sincerity.

Dex unbuckled his belt and balanced it carefully onto the top of the end post of the stall where he'd been told, then added the other big Webley too. Dammit.

"Now, mister. You come out here. You and me, we will play the game, the two of us together."

Dex gave the brown horse a reassuring pat, then opened the stall gate and stepped out into the aisle to meet Luis and his wicked blade.

· 25 ·

They had him cold, these two, and almost certainly thought of him as being as good as dead. Yet it was not fear that Dex was feeling as he stepped out to meet them. And, recognizing that, it actually puzzled him for a moment. Probably he should be afraid. Probably he should be terrified.

Instead he felt . . . he had to think about it for a brief moment . . . exhilarated. That was it.

This ugly experience was not at all what he would consider to be fun. But it was damned sure exciting. Almost—almost but not exactly—enjoyable.

Thrilling, he supposed would be one way to think of it.

His heart rate increased and he felt a tightening of the flesh across the nape of his neck and down onto his shoulders.

In a way he was very nearly looking forward to the dangers yet to come and to the release that movement and action would give him.

Dex found himself smiling.

"You think something is funny, Yankee?" Luis asked.

"I'm not a damnyankee, remember."

"Oh, yes. My apologies, señor." Luis was grinning, eager. Dex gathered that the fellow liked this sort of thing.

Well, they'd just have to see how well he liked it when it was over.

"Nice knife," Dex said. "Mind if I use a stick when we play this game of yours?" He picked up the cane from the front wall of the stall where he'd left it minutes earlier.

"You think you can stop Luis with that?" Luis asked. Dex always kinda wondered about people who referred to themselves in the third person. He always suspected that their hinges were a few pins short of being complete.

"I'd certainly like to try," Dex responded.

"Si, señor, you do that. Make my game more fun, I think."

"Hell, Luis, let me shoot the son of a bitch an' let's be done with it," the Anglo suggested. It was not an offer that Dex much appreciated.

"No, I want to do this. We play the game. Have some fun. I 'ave done this many times. This time, *si*. Could be very good. You jus' stand back an' let me do, eh?"

"Whatever you say, Luis."

Luis grinned at him and bowed, then sucked in his belly and rose onto his toes, posturing as if he were a matador preparing to taunt the bull. He held his slim knife overhead, the tip of the blade pointed stiffly toward Dex's throat.

Dex saluted him with the cane and lowered it.

"Huh. Huh." Luis's grunt was low-pitched and harsh, again as if the man were a matador in the ring. He danced backward, inviting a charge.

Dex laughed and, feeling genuinely eager, dropped into a half crouch and glided swiftly to his left, his eyes locked on Luis, both hands clutching the cane that he held straight out in front of him.

Neither Luis nor the Anglo seemed to notice that Dex's movement took him between the two men and quite close to the tall Anglo with the Colt revolver. Both of them were concentrating on Luis and his pretty knife.

Dex, on the other hand . . .

Once he had the position he wanted, Dex held the barrel

of the cane steady with his left hand, holding Luis's attention there.

With his right, though, he slipped the sword blade free of its wooden containment and in the same swift motion slashed the sharp edge of the blade—his blade, dammit, a good three times longer than Luis's—across the knuckles of the Anglo's gun hand.

The man screamed as blood spurted and his revolver fell to the straw-littered floor of the livery stable.

The gun was not the only thing that dropped. So did three, pink, twitching sausages of flesh, the Anglo's severed fingers.

The would-be gunman dropped to his knees, clutching his maimed right hand in his left.

Dex misinterpreted the movement. His first thought was that the Anglo was trying to snatch up his gun with his undamaged left hand. It was an unlucky thought. Unlucky for the Anglo, that is, because the next sweeping flash of Dex's sword cut across the man's neck and laid open the big artery there.

Fresh gouts of blood flew high into the air, and the Anglo fell over.

By the time the Anglo hit the ground, Dex had spun back to face a suddenly pale Luis.

"Now," Dex said, "let's play that game of yours."

• 26 •

"I'm sorry, Marshal, but that's about as good a description as I can give you. Well, that and the fact that this Luis can run almighty fast." Dex barked out a short, harsh laugh. "The last thing I saw of him was butt and boot heels. He was making tracks hard and fast in that direction." He pointed.

Marshal Harris seemed to find less amusement in the situation than Dex did. But then the marshal wasn't the one who'd just faced death and came away unscathed. The simple fact of it was that Dexter was feeling very pleased with himself.

"The two of them obviously knew each other. I'd say they were friends. So if you know who this one is you should be able to find the other one easily enough," Dex suggested, looking down toward the livery stable floor where the Anglo's body lay now in a pool of sticky, clotting blood. Dex hadn't known there could be that much blood in one man's body. And flies? Every fly in a fifteen-mile radius must have gotten the word about the free lunch being offered for them here. He could hear the low, buzzing drone as they landed, swarmed about through the air and went back to drink some more.

"I'm afraid I don't know anyone named Luis," Harris said. "Not one that looks like you say this knife man did anyway. And I've never seen this jehu in my life. He's not from Winter Grove."

Dex frowned. "I was kind of assuming that this one would be Blake's man Joshua Bonner."

"Nope," the marshal said. "Bonner is shorter than this fellow was and wears a beard. And if there was killing to be done, I can't imagine Josh Bonner letting anybody else do it for him. Killing is the sort of work I suspect he would enjoy."

"But if this isn't Bonner . . ."

Tom Harris shrugged. "It beats me, Mr. Yancey. You say they made no attempt to rob you and said nothing about money. Can you think of anyone else who might hold something against you? Something serious, I mean?"

"No, of course not."

Harris grunted softly and said, "Check his pockets, Henry. Let's see if we can figure out who this man was and why he would want to waylay our visitor here."

Deputy Langley's expression suggested that he did not relish the task, but an order was an order. And obviously the marshal did not want to be the one to step in all that blood and gore. Langley practically tiptoed his way into the dark red puddle, raising great swarms of angry flies with every movement. Before rifling the pockets of the recently deceased he had sense enough to drag the body out of the accumulation of blood. Dex helped to the extent of laying down an armful of straw, and Langley deposited the dead man there.

"Eleven dollars and change," Langley reported over his shoulder as he went. "Pocket knife. Little bag of . . . let me see." He opened the leather pouch, looked inside and leaned down to sniff of the contents. "Tobacco. Real cheap tobacco." He went back to his investigations. "Pipe. Box of sulphur matches. Piece of silver here. Looks like it's a twenty-five-cent piece that he's been tapping around the edges to turn into a ring. Not finished though. Folded-over sheet of paper." Langley made a very sour face and held the next article up with only the tips of two fingers. "Handkerchief. Used. Used a lot."

"Let me see the paper," Harris said. "Maybe that will tell us who he was." A moment later the marshal reported, "This doesn't say anything about who the man was, but it does tell us why he wanted you dead, Mr. Yancey."

"You have the goods on Blake now? Fine."

The marshal shook his head. "Had nothing to do with Curtis Blake nor Josh Bonner, either one, Mr. Yancey."

"But if they didn't . . ."

"Ever hear of a," the marshal glanced down at the flyer in his hand, "Mrs. Jane Carter of Galveston, Texas?"

"Damn!" Dex snapped.

"You do know her then."

"I knew a Jane Carter, sure. She wasn't living in Galveston at the time, but I don't suppose that matters."

"Apparently not. Whatever you did to this woman, Mr. Yancey, it was enough to make her post a reward of five thousand dollars in gold coin to whoever brings her your head." The marshal sounded slightly puzzled when he added, "This poster says there will be a bonus payment if the head is delivered wrapped in the hood of a Loyal Knight. Whatever the hell that means. You must really have made this woman angry, Mr. Yancey."

"I did nothing illegal, Marshal, although she and her husband certainly were trying to."

"I see. Sort of."

"I'd heard she was putting a price on me, but that was a while back and a long way from here. I didn't think I'd have to worry about that again."

"If it were me, Mr. Yancey, I would worry."

"Let's hope it was an aberration, Marshal. Luis is a knife man. I doubt he would want to face a gun. And he knows I'd recognize him if he came near me again. I think I'm safe enough." Dex sighed.

"Shall I repeat my advice to you, Mr. Yancey?"

"Don't bother, Marshal. Is there going to be any, um, inquest about this or any charges?"

"Not as things stand right now. I'll be looking into it, of

course. I'll want to speak with Jimmy Payne, of course. He doesn't often leave his stable here during the day. He might be able to tell me something. And I'll want to know if anyone in town has seen this man and the Mexican together. But unless I find something to make me reverse my opinion about your story, I wouldn't think you have to worry about charges being filed."

"I'm free to go now?"

"Yes. Indeed, I hope you will. Permanently."

"Sorry, Marshal," Dex said. He did not mean it.

He had long since retrieved his Webleys and buckled them back into place where they belonged. Now he returned to the stall where James's horse was standing. He made short work of saddling it and slipping James's bridle into place. Even so, by the time he led the brown horse out into the slanting afternoon sunlight, straw had been spread thick over the spilled blood and the Anglo's body had been removed. Marshal Harris gave Dex a perfunctory wave and went back to whatever it was he was doing while he squatted in the middle of the stable aisle with his eyes on the much-trampled ground there.

· 27 ·

It was dark by the time he brought the tired and thoroughly exercised brown to the hitching rails beside Eleanor Adams's whorehouse, and Dex was becoming hungry again. He hadn't thought about that before he rode out of town, dammit. Lately his schedule had been off in too many ways.

Still, food could come later. Right now he wanted to plead for Mrs. Adams's help. He was not entirely sure just how he intended getting C. Julian Blake to back off and let James out of the Winter Grove pokey, but he knew it never hurt to know one's enemy. And Eleanor Adams and her soiled doves were the way to do it.

The black woman, Betty Lou, greeted him at the door and welcomed him inside. "Yessir, Mistuh Yancey, I get her right away. Or is you here to pick one of the young ladies for y'self?"

"I'd like to see Mrs. Adams if it's convenient."

"Yessuh, right away, suh." Betty Lou took Dex's hat, curtsied and hurried upstairs.

Dex fleetingly wondered if Eleanor were, um, *entertaining* up there. She'd said she didn't do that herself. But whores have been known to extend the bounds of truth upon occasion.

And Dex wouldn't mind what she did, really, except if she did entertain a client now and again he damn sure would want to be on that list of acceptable gents. After all, Ellie Adams was one very fine-looking example of the human female. He wanted her and she knew that he did, and it would disappoint him greatly if she refused to take him to bed out of sheer distaste. It wasn't like he had extreme body odor or anything, was it? Or . . . He looked around to make sure no one was watching, then quickly dropped his chin and took a sniff in the vicinity of his armpit. No, dammit, it wasn't that. Although a bath wouldn't do him any harm, actually.

"She be right down," Betty Lou told him. "You can wait back here." The servant led him into Eleanor's office and left him there.

It would have been decidedly rude of him to examine the papers that lay on top of her otherwise tidy desk, and the room was not large enough to take him very far away from the things that were laid out there. He made sure there could be no appearance of impropriety by turning his back on the desk and occupying himself by once again examining the paintings displayed on Eleanor's walls.

They really were quite nicely done. Tasteful. Good brushwork. Nicely composed. He wasn't so sure about the quality of paint that had been used. But then a young lady of upper-class Southern breeding could not be expected to know the ins and outs of paint mixtures the way a professional artist would.

Apart from that minor detail, though, he was quite thoroughly impressed.

He was also smiling very broadly when Eleanor Adams joined him five or six minutes later.

"I know how both of us are going to get what we want from C. Julian Blake," he announced cheerfully. "Sit down and let me tell you about it."

· 28 ·

Marshal Tom Harris was not a happy man. "Damn it, Mr. Yancey, the world is coming to a sorry state when you can't count on a man to lie when you expect him to."

Dex could only grin. "Marshal, I have no idea what you might be talking about."

"Like hell you don't. The only reason I agreed to allow Mrs. Adams to hire my prisoner was so you could sneak out there and the two of you run away."

James had spent the day performing manual labor on Eleanor Adams's property, temporarily freed as a trustee employed by her on behalf of the town. His purported chore had been to dig a well on her waterless homestead, a pursuit that she argued would benefit the town—and make the prisoner hire legal and proper—by extending the supply of available water in this largely arid part of the country.

"You know good and well I expected you and him to run away," the marshal complained now. "I tell you true, Mr. Yancey, I like to keep a calm and orderly town here. And since you and that nigger of yours showed up, one of our leading citizens has had his jaw broken, not once even but twice over, and a man has been killed.

"I'm not saying it wasn't justifiable. I read enough from

the footprints in Jimmy Payne's stable to see that you were telling me the truth the other day."

Which explained what the marshal was doing squatting in the mud there, Dex thought.

"There were two of them, all right, and they came in behind you. Besides, some of the regulars down at the Big Bull Saloon say they saw the two together. Described the Mexican just like you said he was. And they tell me this Luis sat at a table for better than an hour sharpening his knife and humming a little tune under his breath while his friend had some drinks and got himself laid.

"The girl the man went with . . . he said his name was Dave if it makes any difference, which I suppose it doesn't . . . anyway, the girl said he was bragging that he was going to come into big money soon. She figured he was lying, of course. Said half her customers tell her that. Mostly the same ones that try and get her to drop her price. Anyway, it all proves out pretty much like you told me. And there's that poster Dave was carrying when you killed him."

"Successfully defended myself from him if you don't mind," Dex corrected.

"Whatever. Anyway, that one is dead. God knows what happened to the other one. He could still be around someplace. Or some others just like him, wanting that five thousand for your head in a flour sack."

"With a bonus if it's in a Klan hood," Dex pointed out with a grin.

"You aren't taking any of this very seriously," the marshal accused.

"I have to tell you, sir, I'm in much too fine a mood lately to be worried about things that may never happen."

"Yes, and that worries me too. For days now you've been acting like a model citizen. Whistling and chuckling and scratching your ass just as happy as a village idiot. You are up to something, Mr. Yancey, and I will admit to you . . . though if you repeat it to any of the town councilmen I'll accuse you of lying . . . I have to admit to you that I would've been happy as a hog in shit if you and your nigger snuck off from that piece of work and ran far and fast away from my town.

"Damn it, man, that's the reason I let him do that job, you know. If I'd known he wasn't going to run away I would have had him busy filling the ruts and potholes on the public streets here. And there's trash that needs to be hauled off. A water trough to repair and some new hitch rails. There are public works projects that need doing, you know. I could have had him working on those."

"Marshal, I am sorry to disappoint you about this," Dex lied cheerfully.

"You're up to something," the marshal said again. "You and Mrs. Adams too. She's helping you somehow. Damned if I know how. Or what. But you're up to something."

"I am an innocent man, Marshal," Dex said with a completely straight face.

"Yes, and I've heard that one too. Just about every time I lock a man up, in fact." The marshal shook his head and sighed. "Someday, Mr. Yancey, I hope to have the pleasure of arresting a man who admits he's guilty. If I ever do, by God, I think I'll let him go just on general principles."

"Do you need me for anything else, Marshal?"

"No, I do not." He turned and snapped at his deputy, "Henry, let the prisoner go draw some water so's he can bathe himself and clean up some. And don't watch him too close while he's doing it. If he wants to run off, let him. And good riddance."

"Marshal!"

"Oh, hell, Henry, don't get yourself into an uproar. I didn't mean that."

But he did. Dex was sure of it.

And they really did not have to worry about James trying to escape. No sir, they did not.

There were things to be done before Dex and James mounted up and moved on. Yes sir, there most certainly were.

◆ 29 ◆

"More pie, Mr. Yancey?"

"No thanks, Albert. I'm stuffed." Over the past week and a half he'd become a regular at the cafe. Not that the food here was so awfully good. It was just that everywhere else in Winter Grove the food was simply awful. Dex carefully folded his napkin and laid it beside his plate.

"More coffee then?" the waiter/cook/proprietor offered.

"That I would enjoy, Albert. Thank you." It would be several hours before Ellie was awake. The little affair they were engaged in—not the sort of affair Dex would have liked to engage in with her unfortunately—did not take away from her obligations at the whorehouse. She still had to stay awake very nearly the entire night through and sleep during the day. So there was no point in him hurrying the afternoon away, and it had become his habit of late to idle through the afternoons here with coffee and a book.

The town had no library and none of the stores stocked anything more interesting than seed catalogs, but he'd discovered that Marshal Harris's night deputy was an avid reader. The man was pleased to find someone else who appreciated the written word and did not mind sharing his personal collection. At the moment Dex was rereading the works of Tennyson, who was one of his favorites. One of Dex's fantasies was that someday he might meet the great poet. James, on the other hand, was reading a thick volume that claimed to be a true and accurate account of the pirates and bucaneers of the Caribbean. Em Tyler, the owner, seemed to appreciate one of those widely disparate books quite as much as the other.

Dex pushed his cup across the table so Albert could more easily fill it, then looked up as a newcomer entered the restaurant.

"Now don't you be causing any trouble here, Joshua," the restauranteur warned. "Marshal Harris says there's bad feelings between your boss and Mr. Yancey here. I won't be having any rowdiness in my place. You hear me, Joshua? If you're up to trouble, you take it someplace else."

So this, Dex realized, was Joshua Bonner. He'd wondered when Blake's chum would show up.

Now that he had, Dex was not impressed.

Bonner had a bristly beard that was such a bright, pale shade of yellow that it looked like a pasted-on fake. He wore his hair long and had two guns strapped onto his legs. The revolvers hung so low on the man's thighs that Dex thought it a wonder that Bonner could reach them.

He was dressed all in black. Black trousers, black shirt, knee-high black stovepipe boots, black gunbelt, wide-brimmed black hat. Dex gathered that Bonner fancied himself something of a menace and had dressed up especially for the occasion.

"Hello," Dex said pleasantly. "Join me for a cup of coffee?"

"I didn't come here to socialize," Bonner said in a low, growling tone.

Dex smiled at him. "It's good coffee. Sure you don't want some? My treat."

"I already told you I don't, dammit."

"Don't cuss. Albert's little girl is playing in the back. She might overhear. We wouldn't want that."

Bonner looked at Albert and, crestfallen, said, "I'm awful sorry about that. I didn't know."

Dex had no idea if the little girl was in the kitchen or not. But he doubted Albert would correct him if she wasn't.

"Last call for that coffee, Mr. Bonner."

"Dang it, Yancey, I didn't come here for no coffee. Stop inviting me."

"All right, but there's pie still warm from the oven to go with it. I'd take some if it was me," Dex said.

"Mr. Yancey, I came here to call you out. Now you *know* that, don't you."

"Call me out? I don't understand."

"Call you outside. You know. To fight."

"Fight? Why should we fight. Really, Mr. Bonner, we've never met before this moment right now. Are you angry at me?"

"I . . . yes. I am. I'm really mad at you."

"Well in that case, Mr. Bonner, why don't you tell me why you think we should have a fight. If I've done something wrong perhaps I can do something to correct the problem."

"You know you haven't, d . . . darn it." Bonner glanced rather nervously toward the kitchen where the child was supposed to be playing and perhaps listening in. He looked back at Dex. "We're sworn enemies, you and me. And I'm calling you out, mister."

"I see." Dex picked up his coffee cup, blew on the steaming surface and took a cautious sip. "Perfect, Albert. I surely do like your coffee. It's a darn shame Mr. Bonner won't have some. Have you ever tried Albert's coffee, Mr. Bonner?"

"I . . . will you quit changing the subject? Please?"

"I'm sorry." Dex smiled. "Just trying to be friendly, you know."

"You can't get friendly with a man who's calling you out, mister. That ain't right."

"Sorry. Is there some particular etiquette about this?"

"What?"

"Rules. Are there rules that should be followed in an affair of . . . what did you say? . . . calling someone out?"

"Of course there's rules. I call you out, see. Then we

both go outside. We stand in the street a block, two blocks apart facing each other. Then one or the other of us starts walking forward. That's the walk-down, is what they call it."

"Walk-down," Dex repeated. "Uh huh."

"Then when we're close enough, one of us goes for his gun."

"Gun? I thought you said we were going to fight. Like, oh, fisticuffs, I suppose I had in mind. A Marquis of Queensbury prize-fighting sort of thing with a ring and seconds and a line to toe after each round."

"No, no, it ain't nothing like that. This is with guns. Quickest man wins, you see."

"Quickest. All right. But how do we determine who's the quicker? Is there a judge? Do we stand close so one person can see both of us at the same time?"

Bonner was beginning to look just a wee bit exasperated. "Look, Mr. Yancey, this is a shoot-out, don't you see. We shoot at each other. Quickest man wins, see, because the slow one is shot."

"I see," Dex said. He took another sip of the piping hot coffee. "May I ask you something?"

"Yeah."

"You say the first man to shoot is the winner. But what if the second man shoots the straighter of the two? I mean, what if the first man gets his shot off quick, but he misses. Then the slow man shoots him, and the first one dies. Is he still considered to be the winner in this thing?"

"No, Goddammit . . . oh, sorry, Albert . . . sorry there little Sarie, don't you pay no mind to me . . . no, of course the first guy wouldn't be the winner if he's dead, Mr. Yancey. The one that survives is the winner regardless."

"What about if both survive? Like maybe one is wounded. Or both are. Then how do you decide?"

"Goddammit, Yancey, you're trying to confuse me." By now he was so upset that he probably didn't even realize he'd cursed. He certainly did not apologize to Albert or to the little girl who might actually have been there. "Get this straight, mister. I am calling you out. For a duel. With guns. D'you understand that?"

"Yes, that sounds clear enough, Mr. Bonner."

"Fine. Thank you. Now then . . . I am calling you out. I'm gonna go outside now and walk down the street two blocks. When you're ready, you come out too. We'll do the walk-down thing, and when either one of us wants to he can go for his iron an' start the ball to rolling. Is that all right with you, Mr. Yancey?"

"Whatever you say, Mr. Bonner."

"Thank you very much."

"You needn't be sarcastic, Mr. Bonner. I was only trying to understand what you intended."

"Fine. Now you know. D'you have a choice about which end of the street you want?"

"Whatever you prefer will be just fine with me, Mr. Bonner. But I thank you for asking."

"All right then, dammit." Bonner stood there for a moment more, then announced, "I'm going out now."

"That's fine, Mr. Bonner."

"I'll be waiting for you."

"You do that, Mr. Bonner."

"I'm gonna go to that end of the street." He pointed.

"Very well, Mr. Bonner. Thank you for telling me."

"All right then."

Dex thought Bonner looked more than a little frustrated when he finally turned and stalked outside, spurs clanking and guns tied low, a specter—or perhaps more accurately a spectacle—dressed all in black.

"My goodness," Albert said.

"Uh huh." Dex had more coffee. It had cooled enough by now that he could enjoy a swallow rather than settling for a sip. "I surely do like your coffee, Albert."

· 30 ·

"Are you sure you don't want me to go get the marshal, Mr. Yancey? He isn't going to like this, you know. He likes for everything to be lawful and orderly," Albert said nervously.

"No, that won't be necessary, Albert, but thank you for the suggestion. I tell you what, though. There are a couple things I'd like you to do, if you would."

"Sure, Mr. Yancey. If I can."

"Oh, this won't be too much of a burden I shouldn't think. All I want you to do is first to pour me another cup of that good coffee. Then I'd like you to go up and down the street and tell everybody that there's going to be a duel. And make sure you tell all the gents in the saloons. They ought to be interested, don't you think?"

Albert bobbed his head eagerly. "That's all? That's what you want me to do?"

"Yes. And the coffee first if you don't mind."

"It might take me a while to get everybody outside, Mr. Yancey."

"That's all right, Albert. I'm not in a hurry."

"But what about Mr. Bonner?"

Dex shrugged. "If he gets bored standing out there I suppose he could leave."

Albert laughed just a little and went to get the coffeepot from the kitchen.

"I think most everybody in town is lined up along the sidewalks, Mr. Yancey, and Joshua is down at the end of the street getting madder and madder. If he was a steam boiler he'd of exploded half an hour ago."

"You told him I'd be along soon though, didn't you, Albert?"

"Yes, just like you asked me to."

"The marshal is out there still?"

"He sure is. Him and Joshua had words already. Soon as he heard what was going on he came running to see. He's out there close to where Joshua is standing."

"Then I think it's time for me to go see about a walkdown." Dex grinned. "I've never been called out before. You, Albert?"

"Me? Not hardly. To tell you the truth, Mr. Yancey, the only place I've ever heard about this calling-out and walking-down nonsense is in those dime novels some fools back East make up and write about us folks out here in the West."

"Uh huh. I kinda suspected that might be so. Still, improbable or not, it's happened now. I think it's time for me to go meet Mr. Bonner's challenge."

"Yes sir, Mr. Yancey. Good, uh, good luck."

"Thank you, Albert." Dex dropped a silver dollar on the table to cover his meal and then some, retrieved his hat from the rack beside the front door and walked out into what was left of the afternoon's sunlight.

· 31 ·

"You're late," Bonner accused. "And you're supposed to be down at that end of the street, dammit, not sneaking up on me from the crowd like that. I didn't see you coming. How am I supposed to decide when to make my draw if I can't see you walking at me."

"Sorry," Dex told him. "I wanted to clear up a couple things."

Marshal Tom Harris came hurrying over to them. "I'm not going to allow a shoot-out on my streets," he said. "I'll lock you up, both of you, before that happens."

"Goodness, Marshal, we haven't shot anyone," Dex said.

"Besides, Marshal, this is a fair fight," Bonner said.

"Now that's what I wanted to talk to you about, Joshua."

"What's that, Mr. Yancey?"

"Dexter."

"Say what?"

"My name. It's Dexter. You can call me that."

"But I . . ."

"Oh, no one will mind. And I'm sure there isn't anything in the rules about the combatants not calling each other by name. I mean, we can be friendly about this, can't we? We both want to do it right."

Bonner looked more confused than ever. But less angry. The anger seemed to be getting lost amid the clutter. "I guess we do want t' do things right." He gave Dex a sheepish grin and added, "Dexter."

"Thank you, Joshua. That sounds ever so much better."

"What the hell are you two up to here?" the marshal demanded.

"Why, we're trying to work out the rules of this thing."

"Rules? What the hell kind of rules are there in a gunfight?"

"Calm down, Tom, and Joshua will be glad to explain them to you. He was telling me about the rules a little while ago. At first I didn't understand what he meant by 'calling out' and 'walk-down' and all that stuff. But I've finally realized that what we have here is a duel. Isn't that right, Joshua."

"Yes, Dexter, that's it exactly."

"Dueling isn't legal," Harris protested.

"Are you sure about that, Tom? Is there something on the city's books about it?"

"It isn't in the city code. No, I don't believe that it is. But I'm sure dueling is against state law."

"But you say it's okay inside the town limits, right?"

"That isn't what I said at all, Mr. Yancey."

"Dexter. Please, Tom. We're all friends here, aren't we?"

"I don't know what in hell you are up to, Yancey."

"Dexter," Dex corrected again.

"D'you see, Marshal? D'you see what I've been up against this afternoon? I can't hardly get him to make sense. I'm trying to have a nice, simple little gunfight here . . ."

"Duel," Dex said.

"Yeah, right. Duel. I'm trying to have a duel here, everything proper and aboveboard, and Dexter keeps making my head go in circles."

"But the thing is, Joshua, I'm from Louisiana, and in Louisiana we know an awful lot about dueling."

"You do?"

"Lord, yes. You see, if you'd come to me and proposed a duel, why, I'd have known right off how to handle it.

I've fought many a duel before. It was all that talk about calling-out that confused me."

Bonner perked up. "You know about this stuff, hey?"

"Indeed. I promise you."

"And I've promised both of you that I personally will have you locked up and put at hard labor for the rest of your damned lives if you have a shoot-out on my streets. Just look at all the people standing around out here. You could mow down half the population if you aren't careful."

"Oh, I don't think we would either one of us want to do something like that. I know I wouldn't. And I trust my friend Joshua here to be a good shot too. Is that so, Joshua? Are you a good shot with those pistols?"

"Passing fair," Bonner said, "if I do say so my own self."

"I was sure you would be." Dex smiled and patted Bonner companionably on the shoulder. "No, Tom, I don't think you have to worry about that. And besides, I haven't decided for sure yet that we'll be using firearms."

"What do you mean?" the marshal asked.

"What the hell d'you mean?" Bonner snapped, both men speaking at much the same time.

"Now Joshua, I told you that I know quite a lot about the rules of dueling, and one of those rules is that the man who has been challenged . . . in this case that would be me, you see . . . has his choice of weapons."

"Now dammit, Dexter, we're both wearing belly guns, you and me. Of course we'll use pistols. Everybody uses pistols."

"Oh, goodness no. Dueling pistols, revolvers, swords, knives . . . there are many weapons that a man might honorably and properly choose. One of the favorites along the Mississippi River . . . not among the better classes, mind, but popular . . . is for the men's left hands to be tied tight together and each given a dagger for his right hand. I've personally seen three fights like that." He hadn't. But he did hear of such a thing. Once. "In one of them both men died with their bellies split open and their guts spilling out. Very bloody. But it makes for an exciting duel, I can tell you that."

"That ain't proper," Bonner said.

"Of course it is," Dex said with a gentle smile. "It's in the rules."

"No swords though," Bonner said quickly. "That wouldn't be fair. I heard about you sticking that fella with your sword a couple days ago. You know how to use one of them things and I've never touched one in my whole life. Swords wouldn't be fair."

"No," Dex agreed, "that would not be fair. But it would be within the rules." He paused and appeared to be in deep thought. Then shook his head. "No, Joshua, I just haven't decided yet. That's what was taking me so long back there at the cafe, you see. I've been trying to decide how we should fight. What do you think, Tom?"

"Don't think you're going to rope me into going along with this foolishness," the marshal snapped.

"I know you like your revolvers, Joshua, but do you have any alternate suggestions?"

"Al-ter-what?"

"Alternate. Other. Do you have any other weapons to suggest?" Dex brightened and snapped his fingers. "Maces. We could fight with maces, Joshua. Those would fall under the rules. And it wouldn't endanger any spectators. What do you think, Tom? Surely there is nothing in the town code about gentlemen squaring off with maces."

"What the hell is a mace?" Bonner demanded.

Dex told him.

The would-be gunfighter looked quite thoroughly horrified. "You want me to stand out here in the middle of the street an' we flail away at each other with big damn clubs?"

"We like to call them maces, not clubs. But that would be a rather accurate assessment otherwise." Dex smiled broadly.

"Marshal!" Bonner bleated in a pleading tone.

"I'm sorry, Joshua, but Dexter is right. The mace is an allowable weapon of choice. And he is the challenged party."

"But . . ." Bonner looked frazzled. His gaze swept nervously up and down the street, where by now virtually the entire community had turned out to watch the coming battle. "I'd make a damn fool of myself, Marshal."

"Joshua," Harris pointed out, "you've already *done* that."

"Goddammit, Dexter, I'm not going to go to whacking and being whacked with any damn, spiked club. That ain't . . . it isn't civilized, that's what it ain't."

"I'd be happy to let you withdraw your challenge, Joshua. And to show there's no hard feelings, I'd like to buy you that pie and coffee we talked about a little while ago."

Bonner looked like he'd already been bonked on the head with a mace. But with the encouragement of the marshal and to the great disappointment of at least some of the townspeople he allowed himself to be cozened off the street and back to the cafe.

Dex was as good as his word. He stood good for pie and coffee for both of them.

Joshua Bonner had seconds.

· 32 ·

"Do you know something."

"What's that?"

"You're so cute I can hardly stand it."

Ellie rolled her eyes and threw her hands in the air. "Dexter. Get serious. Please."

"Oh, but I am serious."

"I'm a perfect mess and you know it."

"I never said you were perfect," he laughed. "But you do come kind of close, at that."

She pretended to be annoyed. But he noticed that she quite unconsciously pushed back some wisps of hair that had strayed onto her cheek.

"What do you think?" she asked, straightening up and bending backward from the waist to ease an ache in her back. She'd been bending over a too-low table for the past several hours and was likely feeling the effects of it.

"You're getting there," he said after a moment of critical inspection. "But the angle isn't quite right. There. And over there. Doesn't look, well, entirely natural. You know what I mean?"

Ellie frowned and circled slowly around the table, assessing her creation from different angles, stopping here to tilt her head, there to crouch and look at it from down low.

She really was very cute indeed, Dex thought, as he watched her move, so intent on what she was doing that she was oblivious to his presence. For the moment. The more he was near her the more he wanted to change that state of affairs.

Her neck and one cheek were coated with a fine, white dust, and there was a smudge of something dark and greasy over her left eyebrow. Cute in spite of that, he considered.

"Did you know . . ." he started in, intending to amuse and—hopefully—to move his case forward with this lovely, auburn-haired widow. His comment was interrupted by a polite but insistent tapping on the door to Ellie's office.

"Excuse me, Dexter."

He gave her a formal bow, only half in jest while the other half was a reminder to her of his station and upbringing; Ellie was a Southern girl herself and would be much more apt to accept a well-bred Southern gentleman into her bed than, say, a damnyankee.

Betty Lou was at the door. She went onto tiptoes to whisper something into Ellie's ear, then glided silently away.

"Excuse me, Dexter. I'll not be long," Ellie said. Then she left too, latching the door shut behind her.

Dex helped himself to a tot of brandy, then wedged himself into a corner of the room, which was the only available space remaining in the office. He sat and contemplated the object Ellie Adams had been laboring over.

He just wished he knew where they were going with this business. It was his idea, after all, and the truth was that he was still feeling his way through the details. Like . . . just how in hell were they supposed to do it.

He knew well enough where he wanted to go. It was only the "how to get there" part that he was still hazy with.

"Something wrong?" Dex asked when Ellie returned. She hadn't been gone long.

"Not really. Marguerite and Carole Anne are back, that's all."

That was not anything close to being all. He could see

that plain enough in the look she gave him. Her expression was much like that of a cat with bright yellow canary feathers in its whiskers.

"I see," Dex said solemnly. "And where, may I ask, have Marguerite and Carole Anne been?" He wasn't sure of the time but he judged it would be in the neighborhood of two o'clock in the morning.

"They've been entertaining Curtis Blake. In his home. The poor man isn't feeling up to going out anywhere yet." She laughed. "And they said he's even grumpier than usual. I gather he's really quite pissed off because Dr. Stuart won't allow him to drink as long as he's still taking laudanum for the pain, so he's angry about that. And he's furious that he can't eat. Doc prescribed eggnogs for nourishment. He can only take liquids and has to drink them through a glass laboratory tube. It must be awful."

"Somehow I'm not feeling very sympathetic yet. But do go on," Dex invited.

"And of course one of the things that really distresses him is that if he tries to romp one of my girls, that jostles him and makes the pain worse."

Dex laughed aloud at that sad news.

"All he can do is lie still while they, um, attend to things."

"Well, that can be fun too," Dex suggested. "Would you like a demonstration?"

"Are you suggesting that I do you?" Ellie asked. He couldn't honestly tell from her voice if she resented the idea . . . or might possibly be considering it. "Or did you want to do me?"

"Both," he told her with a smile.

"You really should learn to be more serious, Dexter."

"Oh, but I am."

"Pshaw!"

"If you think so. But it's an open offer."

Ellie drew back and gave him a searching look. For a moment there . . . But the moment passed and she said, "The only thing my girls learned tonight is that Curtis fired Joshua Bonner." She smiled. "Apparently making friends with you . . . and being seen in public doing it . . . was not at all what Curtis wanted the poor man to do. In a way, Dexter, I feel sorry for Joshua. He had a lot of the town fooled into thinking he was such a hard man. But he isn't. He is . . . impressionable, I would say. And not really all that bright. He just did whatever Curtis told him to. And he tried so awfully hard to be like those gun-carrying desperadoes that he reads about in those silly books. Now people are getting a better look at the real Joshua. I think they'll learn to like him more than they did before, but I'm afraid this has cost him his job."

Dex rubbed his chin—at this late hour he was in need of a shave again; wouldn't it be a shame if he were to scrape Ellie's soft, soft cheek with those prickly whiskers; wouldn't it be fine indeed if he were to be able to—then he smiled. "Don't feel sorry for Joshua," he said. "I know where he'll find work now."

"Mmm?" Ellie was scarcely paying attention. Her concentration was already back on the project that occupied most of her office floor space these days.

"You're going to hire him," Dex informed her.

"I *beg* your pardon?" Her attention returned quite fully to him. "Have you forgotten that it is really Curtis who pays the salaries around here? Including mine?"

"Haven't forgotten that at all, ma'am."

"Then perhaps it's escaped your attention that I have no money to hire him with. Nor for that matter any need to hire him. What possible work could he do around here, Dexter?"

Dex grinned. "I didn't say he'd be working here, did I? What I *am* thinking is that this would be a good time to hire a man to guard the, um, old homestead and that well James started digging for you."

"But . . ." She stopped. Her brow furrowed, then quickly smoothed again as comprehension came to her. "Oh." She laughed and clapped her hands. "Of course we should have a guard."

"I'll pay his salary. But he's not to know that," Dex said.

"Of course not." Ellie giggled. "This really could be fun couldn't it, Dexter?"

"Yeah. Yeah, I'd say that it could be at that," he agreed.

❖ 33 ❖

"Join me, Marshal?" Dex kicked an empty chair away from his table and motioned for Albert. "What would you like?"

"Coffee, please."

"No pie?"

Harris patted his belly and shook his head. "At my age a man has to slow down." He sighed. "About 'most everything."

"Were you looking for me, Marshal?"

"No, I wasn't, Mr. Yancey, but now that I've found you I do have some questions that I'd like to ask. If you wouldn't mind."

Dex shrugged. "I have nothing to hide from the law, Marshal. Ask anything you like." He added a grin and said, "I might even tell the truth."

Albert brought a cup for Tom Harris and a refill for Dex. The marshal waited until he had gone back to his kitchen before he spoke again. "There are some very strange goings-on out at the Widow Adams's place. I was wondering what you might know about that."

Dex laughed. "Marshal, I expect there are really strange things that go on in that house nearly every night. But if you want a customer list kept, you'll have to get it from a better source than I am."

"That isn't what I want, and you know it."

"Do I, Marshal?"

"I'm sure you do, Mr. Yancey. And that isn't all I know. I know you spend a great deal of time out in Mrs. Adams's relaxation palace."

"No crime in that, I hope."

"No, and I wouldn't be curious about it except I understand you never take any of the girls upstairs."

"Now how would you know a thing like that, Marshal?"

Harris didn't answer him. He only sat there looking Dex straight in the eyes and patiently waiting for that calm expectancy to drive an explanation into the open.

It was a common enough trick, part of a game that Dex didn't particularly feel like playing at the moment. He was willing to let the marshal stew in silence the rest of the afternoon if the man so chose. Instead Dex occupied himself with blowing on his coffee and very carefully sipping from the dark, aromatic . . . something occurred to him as he peered into the depths of the coffee cup. But it was something that would have to wait until later. Much later. Right now he had a guest to entertain.

"Sure you wouldn't like to change your mind about that pie, marshal?" Dex was in a decidedly good mood now that the answer to a vexing problem had presented itself.

"It isn't the activity in the house that interests me anyway, Mr. Yancey. Like you say, there is no crime in that. But I am very curious about the things that seem to be happening out at the old Adams homestead."

"Really? How's that?"

"That is what I was hoping you could explain. Why is Mrs. Adams all of a sudden wanting a well dug? And if she is going to dig a well, why way back at the ruins of that old soddy instead of putting it close by the house? As it is she has to carry water out from town to fill the cistern at the house. Even if she made a new well at the soddy she would still have to haul water. The distance couldn't be much different. If anything I'd say the old house might even be farther than the town well."

"Have you asked her about this, Marshal?"

"Right now I'm asking you, Mr. Yancey."

"Goodness, why should I know anything about it?"

"And that is a good question too, isn't it," Harris said. "Why should you indeed? Yet your nigger was hired to do the digging. She was adamant that she get a prisoner to do the work cheap. Went so far as to get some of the town council to support her request. And of course your man was the only prisoner I had at the time. Makes me think she wanted him in particular, and I know you were out there talking with him when he was working."

"I never tried to hide that, Marshal. What would you expect? The man is my friend. Of course I enjoyed a chance to talk with him when there were no iron bars between us."

"But you didn't try to run away with him. I told you before, the only reason I let him go on the work detail was because I hoped you'd both run just as far from my town as you could get.

"And Mrs. Adams . . . I doubt she saved fifty cents in the cost of labor by hiring a town prisoner instead of giving the work to one of the layabouts at the saloons. Hell, man, she could have gotten the work done free for nothing if she'd offered to pay in trade instead of cash. So why'd she want so bad to have your man out there digging that hole in what we all know is dry ground?"

"The way I understand it, Marshal, she had a customer who's a diviner. He took a willow switch and located the spot for her. Said she'd be sure to find sweet water not more than twenty feet down if she dug right at that place."

"Yeah, I heard that story too, Mr. Yancey. I bet half the men in town have because all the girls at the whorehouse are telling it. What I haven't heard is who this fellow is who divines water and where I can find him to talk to."

Dex shrugged and didn't offer an explanation. That is another trap John Law likes to use when he's talking to a man. Saying too much when you don't have to is suspicious in itself and can too often trip a man up by stringing too

many lies together. A truly fine liar—which Dexter Lee
Yancey considered himself to be—has to have an excellent
memory. One of the things he has to remember is to use
his lies judiciously for too many of them can be as damaging as too few.

"Another thing that makes me curious, Mr. Yancey, is
why Joshua Bonner would be sitting out there now guarding that tumble-down sod house and a dry well."

"Dry is it? I didn't know that was decided already," Dex
said.

"All right. I don't know that either. But I think it is a
pretty safe assumption. And you haven't said a word about
why she wants to have a guard posted out there. God knows
the place has been sitting there abandoned ever since Ned
died. Why would she think someone would be interested
in it now?"

Again Dex only shrugged and kept his mouth shut save
for the introduction of a little coffee into it.

"I know you know something about this, Mr. Yancey,
because Joshua turned the lady down when she first tried
to hire him. I understand you talked him into taking the
job. Now why would you do a thing like that, I've asked
myself."

"Marshal, I was just trying to do two favors at once there.
As you've already mentioned, I am well acquainted with
Mrs. Adams. I like her. She mentioned she wanted a guard,
and I was the one who suggested Joshua. And before you
ask, the reason I thought of him was that I'd heard he lost
his job with Mr. Blake. And I kind of like the fellow. He's
strange, but he's harmless."

"Harmless," Harris snorted. "You wouldn't have thought
Joshua so damned harmless if he'd drawn on you that day.
You don't know how fast he is with those tied-down guns
of his. I've seen him draw, Mr. Yancey. You would've
been a dead man if you'd let him draw on you that day."

"Would I, Marshal?" Dex countered with amusement
rather than alarm.

"Yes, you would. Like I said, I've seen that man draw a
gun. He's unbelievably quick."

Dex chuckled and took a swallow of his coffee. "Ever see him shoot, Marshal?"

"What do you mean?"

"I mean just that. You said you've seen his draw. Ever see him shoot those guns?"

"Mmm, no, I suppose I probably haven't. Joshua liked showing off his speed with a gun. No one around here has ever challenged him. They all know better."

Dex grinned again. "Ever see a man killed by a fast noise, Marshal?"

Harris stared at him.

"When I took Joshua out to see the place he'd be guarding, we had a real nice talk. About guns and calling people out and dime novels. Things like that. He wanted to show me how fast he is. He's proud of that. But I don't think our friend Joshua will be quite so belligerent in the future, Marshal. Nor quite so cocky. You see, after he showed off his draw, Joshua and I had a little contest. We set some clods of dried clay up on what was left of the hog pen out there, and we both drew and fired at the same time to see whose clump of dirt would get busted first.

"Joshua got himself a bit of a surprise out there. You see, he fired a good half second before me every time we drew. Maybe longer than that. Like you say, he's uncommonly quick with that Colt of his. The thing is, though, his bullets never came within ten feet of the mark. And if I do say so, it didn't take me much time to powder my target. I beat him every time, Marshal. Hands down. It shook him up, let me tell you.

"And I hope you'll appreciate that from now on I don't think Joshua will be going around wearing black clothes and putting peroxide in his beard."

"He did that? Damn! I always wondered."

"He did. But I think I've talked him out of that nonsense. On the other hand I may've done something bad too. I think he's going to be doing a lot of target shooting while he's staying out there at the old house for Mrs. Adams. If he practices his aim as diligently as he worked on his speed, our friend Joshua could become formidable if he's ever in a real gunfight. Which, by the way, he never has been. Not once."

"I'll be damned. I always thought . . ."

"Sure. Everybody did. Now if you'll excuse me, I need to see to some things." Dex dropped a coin on the table to pay for his meal and the marshal's coffee, then got out of there before Harris got around to realizing that Dex had shifted the subject from Ellie Adams and her well to Joshua Bonner and his gunfighter fantasies.

Tom Harris was among the people he liked in this town, and Dex would rather not have to spin any more lies for the man than were necessary.

He was whistling to himself as he ambled down the street on his way to the barber's for a shave, a late-day shave so he wouldn't have such sharp stubble on his face this evening. Just in case he could get Ellie to change her mind.

⋄ 34 ⋄

"Coffee," Dex said.

"What about coffee?"

He pointed to the misshapen lump of limestone that occupied most of the floor space in Ellie's office these days. "We soak it in coffee. Pull it out every once in a while. When it gets to a color we like, we just wash it off and put on the finishing details."

"You're a genius," Ellie squealed.

"I know that. I didn't think you were aware of it though," he said with a broad grin.

"I could just kiss you," she declared.

Dex's expression turned immediately serious. "I wish you would," he said in a very soft voice.

"Oh, Dexter, I . . ." She did not finish the sentence, merely shook her head.

Dex stepped in closer and put his arm around her waist. Beneath the loose cloth of her housedress she was very slim, he found. She had a tiny waist but with a full swell of bosom and buttocks. A perfect hourglass, as they said. Except in Ellie's case she really was.

"You know I'm crazy about you," he whispered, his lips

close to her ear so that she would feel the warmth of his breath there. "And . . . you know."

"You can have any of the ladies. I wouldn't charge you. You could have two of them at once. Three if you like."

"What it is going to take for you to realize that I don't want any of your girls. Ellie, I wouldn't want *all* of them at the same time. Not since I had that first look at you sitting so proud and defiant in that buggy. I'm . . . Ellie, you're a Southern girl. A Southern *lady*. How could I think of being with any other girl now that I've gotten to know you."

He kissed her, his embrace close and his hunger for her ragged in his breathing.

Deliberately he pressed his body tight against hers so she could not fail to feel the hard, throbbing proof of his desires and his needs.

Ellie melted to him. Her lips parted, and he explored her mouth with the tip of his tongue.

He could feel her breath quicken, felt her arms slide over his shoulders and around his neck.

She arched her back, responding fiercely now to his kisses.

Then, abruptly, she jerked backward, snatching herself away from him and pushing against his chest with both hands.

Her face was flushed with desire, and he knew she was as randy and ready as he was. Yet she pushed him away with an anguished shake of her head.

She stared at him for a moment and then, turning, fled from the office and the incomplete project he'd dreamed up.

A moment later Dex could hear the sharp, pounding thump of her footsteps as Ellie raced upstairs and far out of his reach.

Dex drew in a series of long breaths, taking the air deep into his lungs and forcing himself to exhale slowly. He was trembling slightly, and his erection was like marble, dammit.

He was tempted to march out there and grab one of the

girls. She'd offered them. Any or all of them.

But he knew what Ellie would think of that if ever he accepted the offer. He would get laid, sure. Probably very expertly too.

But . . . he meant what he'd told her. Now that he knew Ellie, he did not want any of her whores.

It was the Widow Adams that Dexter wanted. Not some hired substitute.

· 35 ·

"I've brought ten pounds of ground coffee," Dex said to
Ellie two days later. He smiled. "Had to go to three stores
in order to buy all we need without raising any eyebrows,
but I think that part of it is all right. The biggest remaining
problem will be finishing this thing without anyone being
the wiser. We can't let anybody know, Ellie. Not even
Betty Lou. And we *certainly* can't let any of the working
girls find out about any part of it or Blake will start getting
suspicious. That will happen soon enough anyway. We
don't want him getting wise until it's too late for him to
do anything about it."

"I assume you have something worked out already or we
wouldn't be having this conversation," she said.

"I do," he admitted. "We have to soak this this thing in
a tub. I assume you have a tub in your private quarters?"

"Yes, of course."

"Big enough to hold our little friend here?"

She nodded. "I'm sure it is."

"So we'll fill it with coffee. Enough liquid to completely
immerse it, anyway. The tub needn't be literally full, just
full enough. We'll have to do that upstairs in your room.
There isn't space enough to bring a tub down here. Not in

addition to the rest of the furniture, and if we moved that out the tongues would wag. There would be some who wondered why. So the best thing will be to take our friend upstairs and put 'er into the tub. Then we can boil the coffee and do the soaking.

"We'll want to do all that . . . moving everything and getting the coffee ready, all of that sort of thing . . . when the girls are asleep so none of them peaches to the fact that things aren't all as they seem. I was thinking that during the forenoon would be the best time. That's when the girls should be sleeping their soundest. If we wait too long some of them will be starting to stir."

"That sounds good," Ellie said.

"What I figure is that I'll spend the night here too. Your girls will notice, of course. But they're sure to already think that you and I are . . . well . . . you know."

Ellie nodded. And blushed. He could hardly believe that. Here the woman was, a grown widow and the madam of a high-class whorehouse to boot. And she *blushed* at the thought of her own whores thinking she was having an affair.

Dex thought that nigh incredible. Charming, sort of. But incredible nonetheless.

"Yeah, well, like I was saying, they already think we're doing something more than playing whist inside this locked office night after night. They're bound to. There won't be any damage to your reputation if I go upstairs to spend the night instead of going back to my hotel for a change."

"No, I . . . suppose it won't hurt at that." She paused and in a small, rather hopeful voice suggested, "Couldn't you stay here in the office instead while I go up to my own room as usual?"

Dex shook his head. "We don't want to do anything that would be suspicious, and now that they think we are having this fling it would only confuse things and get them to wondering if we both spent the night under the one roof but not sleeping together. Besides, with all the clutter in here right now there wouldn't be any place for me to get any sleep, and I'll be needing my rest come the morning.

It's really best if we stay in one place, and that place rightly ought to be in your private rooms."

"I suppose so," Ellie reluctantly agreed.

Dex spent a moment inspecting the article they'd both—well, Ellie for the most part—worked so hard on over the past days. "I think we're ready. Shall we do it tonight?"

"No. Please. I want . . . I want to get used to the idea. You don't mind, do you?"

Dex smiled at her. "You know I couldn't begrudge you anything you asked." He leaned forward and kissed her very lightly. It was not a brotherly kiss exactly. He tasted gently of her lips. But he did not press her about it. "Tomorrow?" he asked.

Ellie nodded. "Tomorrow."

Dex was tempted to kiss her again. He'd been more than a week without release, and he was so horny by now that he hurt.

But trying to lift her skirt now would only ruin his chances for the future, and he knew it.

Didn't like it worth a damn. But he accepted it.

"Tomorrow," he said softly. Then turned and got the hell out of there before he changed his mind and tried to shove his tongue halfway down her throat.

♦ 36 ♦

Dex took his horse for a brisk canter the following afternoon. It needed the exercise, and he needed the diversion of having something—anything—to do. They were getting down to the final details now, and he was more nervous than he would have liked to admit.

If he'd figured this wrong, it would fizzle like a wet candle and James would be spending the next five months in Tom Harris's jail.

But if it soared like a kite instead . . . Dex had his fingers crossed. And his toes. Hell, he'd cross his eyes too if he thought that would do any good. He wanted James out of that jail.

He also wanted Ellie Adams out of debt.

And it wouldn't hurt Dex's feelings the least bit if he could accomplish both those things by putting some egg onto Curtis Blake's face. That would make it all the better indeed.

He took the horse in a wide swing north out of town, then east and in a long loop back until he finally came out on the dry and barren flat where Ned Adams tore up the grass in order to go bust trying to raise grain crops without water. Helluva country, Dex thought. But just the thing if a man loved dust. Yessir, it was just the ticket for that.

He dropped back to a slow walk a couple hundred yards south of the sagging and partially weather-melted sod house that had been Ellie Adams's home here until Blake built the whorehouse for her to run.

Dex was not surprised, though, that she'd stayed here and tried to stick things out rather than go back home as both a childless widow and a failure. Southern girls have a gracious plenty of pride even when they have nothing else at all.

He wondered if Joshua would spot him coming in or if their "guard" was inside snoring.

Dex felt halfway ashamed of himself for the thought when he was still a good hundred fifty yards out. Joshua popped up from where he'd been hiding on the roof of the soddy and stood, calling out Dex's name and waving him in. Joshua was armed with his revolvers and a saddle carbine too, and Dex had little doubt that Bonner was doing the job he'd been hired for here. He was also, Dex noticed, wearing ordinary clothing. The black, dime novel gunfighter outfit was no longer in evidence.

"Howdy, Dex. Can I cool your horse out for you?"

"Hello, Joshua. No need for you to do the walking for that. I can handle it."

"It'd please me to take him for you. Besides, it'd feel good if I could walk around a bit myself. Been laying up on that roof pretty steady."

"On the roof? All damn day?"

Joshua took Dex's reins and began leading the horse slowly around the yard. Dex walked along beside him.

"Through the nights too," Joshua chattered while they walked. "I can see an' hear better up there. An' the grass up there is softer than the slats on the bunk indoors. So I lay up there and doze. But don't you worry. I wake up real often and take a look and a listen. Mostly I only come down to cook something or to take a shit."

"That's too much for one man, Joshua. I wonder if Mrs. Adams would hire somebody to spell you. Like at night or something."

Bonner's face fell. "You think I'm not doing good here, Dex?"

"Joshua, I think you're doing great here. I'm real proud of the job you're doing. I just don't want to ask too much of you. I meant to say . . . I don't want Mrs. Adams to take advantage of you. We're friends, you and me, and I wouldn't like anybody to do that."

Joshua positively beamed when he heard Dex call him a friend. "Don't you worry, Dex. I can handle it. And I don't need help neither. I like it out here. Like it a lot. Want to see how I can shoot now that I been practicing?"

"I'd like to, buddy, but I have to get back to town pretty soon. I have an important appointment tonight, and I have to get a shave and a bath first."

"Next time," Joshua said. If he was disappointed he did not show it.

"You bet," Dex agreed. "Is everything all right out here? You're not having any problems?"

"Nope, no trouble. There was some rattlesnakes nesting in the house, but they weren't much bother. I got the hides staked out over there so's they can dry. Thought I'd make some hatbands out of 'em." His face lighted up with a new thought. "Say, Dex, would you like a snakeskin hatband if I was to make you one?"

"I'd be honored to wear it, Joshua." He wasn't entirely sure about that, but the offer was heartfelt and it would have been rude to reject it. "Any visitors?"

Joshua laughed. "Just one."

"Anybody I know?"

"Prob'ly. It was one o' the whores. Marguerite, her name is. She's pretty. Good fuck too. You ever had her?"

Dex shook his head. "No, but I've heard she's good. I guess Mrs. Adams sent her out, huh?"

Joshua laughed again. "No, 't'wasn't her sent Marguerite."

"Who then?"

" 'T'was Mr. Blake. I'm not s'posed to know that, but I do."

"How's that, Joshua?"

"Marguerite is Mr. Blake's regular snitch. She tells him everything that happens at the house over there. She even spies on Mrs. Adams."

"I didn't know that."

"Oh, sure. I know it 'cause of me working for Mr. Blake too, see. She's always been his spy. I don't know why he'd want to do that, but he does. All the time."

"And you're sure she was checking up on you for Mr. Blake?"

"Sure she was. Marguerite, she used to be uppity. Too good to fuck common folk, see. She never had anything to do with me before, even if I tried to pay her, unless Mr. Blake told her to. Sometimes when he'd be in a good mood with me . . . or when he wanted to do something ugly to punish her by making her do stuff she hated . . . he'd give her to me for a lay. Or sometimes he'd have her lay there while everybody that works for him fucked her. She'd put out then, she would, or get her ass whipped. I know. She tried to say no once. You know what happened?"

Dex shook his head.

"Mr. Blake, he took a whip to her. Not a regular whip but a short one. I think he uses it special for beating on people. And when he was done with that he made her put her mouth on an old dog Mr. Blake brought in out of some alley. I didn't like that. But Mr. Blake, he explained it was just a discipline thing and I shouldn't worry about it. But I didn't like it. Marguerite hated it. And she knows that I saw what she did that time. He had me stay in the room so it would humiliate her all the more. I know she's never forgot that. No, she wouldn't've come out here to wiggle her ass for me unless Mr. Blake told her to. I'm positive about that."

"Did she ask you stuff?"

"Sure. And I done just exactly what you told me t' do if that was ever to happen, Dexter. I told her the truth. Told her the exact an' literal truth, just like you said I should."

"You're a good man, Joshua. I knew I could count on you." Dex clapped his friend on the back and took his reins back from Joshua. "Reckon I should head back now. Thanks for cooling out my horse."

"Anything I can do for you, Dex, you know I'll do 'er."

"I count on that, Joshua." Dex swung onto his saddle and touched the brim of his hat in salute before he wheeled the animal around and set off to town.

• 37 •

Dex stopped by the jail to visit with James before going out to the whorehouse. It was a little early for visiting hours, but Dex and the night man Em Tyler had become fairly chummy since James was locked up. Dex always thought to go to the jail by way of Albert's cafe so he could take a piece of fresh pie to the night deputy.

He was, he reflected, becoming entirely too familiar with Winter Grove and its residents. And, no offense to them, he hoped he could ride on in the *very* near future.

"Everything coming along all right?" James asked. Dex had brought him pie too, and he had to speak around a mouthful of the sweet, runny, many-seeded berries it had been made with.

Dex glanced across the room toward Tyler, but the deputy was devoting his full attention to the dessert. "We're soon ready," Dex said and proceeded to fill him in.

"Do you really think this will work?"

Dex grinned. "No skin off my ass even if it doesn't. I'll just go down to Santa Fe and cozy up to some little ol' Mexican girl with big tits and a warm hole. You can meet me there whenever they get around to letting you out. Well, if they do get around to letting you out, that is. They might get to like you so much they'll keep adding on to the charges against you. I've heard of stuff like that happening, you know."

"Damn but you're a little ray of sunshine, white boy."

"I came here to cheer you up. Try to show some appreciation, will you?" Dex said with a grin. The truth was that he despised having to see James in a jail cell. It gnawed his gut something awful to know that James's freedom was at the whim of some half-assed ignoramus like Justice of the Peace Herbert Grassley.

But then a man has to play the cards he holds. You just can't ask life for a redeal. Unfortunately.

Dex stood—when he'd first started coming here he'd had to stand the entire time of his visits, but now Tyler let him use the stool that usually was beside the heating stove—and said, "I'd best go see if we can start the final phases of this little deal, James."

"Keep your head down, white boy. And when it comes time, strike quick as a snake, you hear?"

"Keep your own burr head down, boy."

Dex spent a few moments making idle conversation with the night deputy—idle, but in fact not at all worthless, because it was this sort of thing that prompted Tyler to warm up to him in the first place—then went outside into the cool of the early evening and headed for the whorehouse.

Tonight, he was hoping.

Hope that had to do with *much* more than his plan to free James.

◆ 38 ◆

They waited until the last of the whores went to bed—well, they'd been going to bed fairly continually throughout the evening—what Dex and Ellie waited for was for the girls to go to *sleep.* They forced themselves to delay another thirty minutes, just to make sure the women would all be sleeping soundly.

After twenty minutes of adhering to that inviolable resolution they couldn't stand it any longer and got started anyway.

"You stir up the fire in the kitchen and get the coffee to cooking. Use the water from the reservoir on the side of the range. It's already hot," Dex reminded her. "Won't take so long to boil."

"Oh, I couldn't do that. There's rust in the reservoir, Dexter. You couldn't make coffee with that."

Dex gave her a look that was half amusement and the other half impatience. "No one is going to *drink* this coffee, Ellie."

"Oh!" She gave him a wide-eyed look and then a little giggle. "You're right. I'll use the stove water."

"Need any extra wood brought in?" he offered.

"We use coal, thank you." She smiled. "We are really

quite modern here, sir. And there is plenty in the bin already. Go on now. You know where to go, right?"

"I know," he said. She must have explained the upstairs layout a dozen times already this evening. But for some reason she hadn't wanted to take him upstairs to show him, which would have been far easier.

While Ellie went off toward the kitchen to begin preparing the gallons of coffee they would need, Dex shook out the sheet she'd brought downstairs—if there is one thing a whorehouse is bound to have in quantity it would be bed linens—and used it to carefully wrap the carved limestone that was the result of all their recent efforts.

If any of the girls was awake and wandering the hallway Dex's presence would be remarkable but not fatal to their plan. But should any of them get a glimpse of the bone-white object the whole purpose would be lost.

He wrapped the stone with the tender care normally reserved for eggs or infants, then strained to pick the damn thing up.

Dex was fit and strong, but it was all he could do to lift the thing. It was heavier than he'd realized.

Once he got it up he tried to rest it against his shoulder, overbalanced and damn near fell. It would have been bad enough to take a tumble. But to drop or somehow break the stone would ruin everything.

He managed to regain his equilibrium, hesitated for just a moment to make sure he had the stone, and himself, under control, then left Ellie's office and started up the stairs.

He left the office door open rather than take the time to pull it closed. This was the first time in—what?—well over a week that the door hadn't been under close lock and key.

Now that they were done with that part of things it would probably take two men and a boy to get the place clean again. But that, thankfully, would be someone else's worry.

Besides. The house really belonged to Curtis Blake, so why should he care if the place was trashed. Fuck 'im.

Dex was staggering, his legs turning quickly to gum rubber, by the time he and his burden reached the top of the stairs and turned toward Ellie's private chambers.

◆ 39 ◆

"It's beautiful," Dex said as he admired the object that lay in Ellie Adams's copper bathtub. There was a good two inches of coffee covering the highest point of stone, but the liquid wasn't so dark that they couldn't see the sculpted shape.

"It did come out rather well, didn't it," Ellie said. "I'd never thought of trying anything like this before, you know. I've always loved art, but the only thing I've done before is paint and make pencil or charcoal sketches. This was . . . it was fun, really."

"You're good at it," Dex said.

"Do you really think so?"

"I do. Seriously."

Ellie sighed. "Why oh why won't the art world take a woman's work seriously?"

"Why oh why," he mimicked, "do you let them keep you out if you want into that world?"

"Because I am a woman, that's why."

"Can I make a suggestion?" he said.

"Certainly, but what's the point? No one can turn a woman into a man, and that is what it would take for my art to be accepted."

Dex touched her arm—her flesh was soft and warm, and he could feel himself growing hard just from that small contact—and said, "Has it never occurred to you that a gallery never need see the artists it represents? I, um, happen to know the owner of a gallery in New Orleans. I could write a letter of introduction." He smiled. "Introducing, say, Mr. E. Z. Adams. You could ship the letter along with a sampling of your work."

"Z?" she asked.

"It has a catchy sound to it, don't you think? Anyway, that isn't the point. I could make the letter introduce you by any name you please. John Smith, for all I care. Your communication with my friend Grayson would all be by mail and freight. Are you interested or not?"

"God, I . . . Dexter, I . . ." She wrapped her arms tight to her chest and shivered. "I never thought about anything like that."

"So think about it. You have until I leave Winter Grove to make up your mind." Never one to let an opportunity pass, Dex moved nearer to her and slipped his arms around here as if to hug and warm her.

Instead he lowered his mouth to hers and kissed her long and deeply.

Ellie's thoughts seemed elsewhere but after only a few seconds he could feel a stirring of interest in her slim body.

More than interest, really. He could feel the beginnings of arousal as her lips parted and her breath quickened.

She returned his kiss with a matching passion of her own, and Dex made sure she could feel the insistent strength of his erection hard against her belly.

He moved so as to pick her up and carry her to the canopied bed at the side of the room.

With a sob that might have been anguish, Ellie stopped him. She pulled stiffly away from him and pushed at his chest to disengage herself from his embrace.

"No," she said, her voice hoarse. Her cheeks were flushed with desire.

He knew she wanted to, dammit. He knew that without any possible room for doubt or dissension.

But her no was firm. He could hear that in her voice too. For whatever reason, she'd chosen to withdraw.

It was her right. He hated it. But it was her right to reject him.

"This, uh, this needs to soak for a while," he said, a bit of a croak in his own voice now as he fought to regain control of his desires. "Why don't we try to get some sleep. I'll, uh, make sure we don't oversleep. Go ahead. Lie down on the bed. I'll curl up on the loveseat over here."

Ellie nodded mutely and turned to walk away from him.

◆ 40 ◆

Dex wakened abruptly, aware of some presence looming over him in the dim, low-trimmed lamplight of Ellie's bedroom.

He had his gun in hand without conscious thought and was embarrassed by this reaction when he saw it was only Ellie standing there.

She recoiled at the sight of the revolver, and he put it hastily away.

"I thought you were asleep," he said.

"I was. I woke up and saw you were sleeping so soundly. I just, well, I thought I would drape an afghan over you or something." The lie was thin. She held no afghan or sheet.

"That's nice of you, thanks."

"I didn't . . . oh, Jesus," she blurted. She stepped half a pace backward and began fumbling at the buttons that held her housedress closed.

She looked about halfway toward crying. But she continued to disrobe until she stood naked before him.

Her body was exquisite. Pale satin flesh molded into subtle swellings and hollows. The lamplight gave her skin a golden glow, and deep shadows hinted of delights that would have to be explored in order to be believed.

Dex stood, so awed and bemused that he reacted as if to a classical sculpture rather than to a real woman. He didn't even have a hard-on.

That state quickly changed when with a sob Ellie came to him. She kissed him and hugged him fiercely. And then she pulled back away from him.

Not in rejection, though. Not this time.

Now she began unfastening the buttons on Dex's clothing.

"Slowly. Please, Dexter. Don't be too quick."

She pressed one hand to his chest while with the other she clung tight to his neck. They lay atop her frilly bed, both naked, both breathing raggedly from passions brought on by the endless kissing and touching that Ellie so obviously wanted.

But now, dammit, if he didn't soon find release, Dex was going to squirt his juice into nothing but empty air. That or spend the next week with his balls aching too hard to let him sit in a saddle. And so he informed her, albeit with slightly different wording.

"Yes, dear. Now. But . . . slowly. Please be slow and gentle with me. Do you . . . must I lick it first?"

"Must you? No, pretty girl, there's no rules here. There's nothing that I'd make you do if you don't want."

"Then just . . . fuck me, Dexter. Please. But slowly. Gently."

He didn't have to say anything. Couldn't at the moment anyway. His mouth was otherwise occupied.

Without breaking the kiss he slid his leg between her knees. Ellie allowed her thighs to part, and Dex moved over her.

His cock was as unyielding as a flagpole and damn near as hard. He could feel the wet heat of her as the head of his dick probed past the thick thatch of dark hair in her vee and found the slippery, dripping opening.

Ellie's breath caught at the feel of him there, and she went tight and tense beneath him.

He held himself motionless above her for several seconds

to allow her to accept him, then pressed forward.

Ellie was tight. He couldn't remember being with a woman this tight—or this hot—in years. So tight that her flesh actually resisted his entry at first, and he pushed a little harder, allowing more of his weight to bear.

He felt the head of his cock find the entry and push through. Felt her body stiffen briefly and as quickly yield to him. Heard her gasp. Felt the heat of her breath in his ear and the incredible heat of her pussy surround and envelop him as, the portal now breached, he slid deep, deep inside Ellie's body.

She cried out and clamped both her arms tight around him.

Dex could feel her passion return and begin its climb toward ever greater heights as soon as he began to gently thrust and withdraw, thrust and withdraw. Slowly at first and then more quickly to keep pace with Ellie's rising excitement.

She began to laugh and then to cry, both the sobs and the muted laughter coming from her throat at the same time, and she reached a trembling—and rather noisy—climax seconds before Dex lost his restraint and plunged hard and fast into her with his own explosive release.

By the time they were done both were limp, sweaty and damned well exhausted.

But Ellie Adams had been worth the wait. Oh, yes, she had. Well worth it, Dex thought.

• 41 •

"I'm all wet and sticky," Ellie said, wrinkling her nose in an expression of distaste. "Ugh."

"Here." Dex plucked a lace-trimmed handkerchief from the bedside table and handed it to her.

Ellie used the hanky to wipe herself and frowned again. Dex glanced down and frowned too when he saw why she'd been even more sticky-wet than one might expect. The handkerchief was bloody.

"You don't . . . dammit, Ellie, you're a widow. You can't have been a virgin." He scowled. "Could you?"

She looked sheepish, as if she'd been caught doing something naughty. "My husband . . . he wasn't well even when we married. He couldn't . . . you know. Couldn't get hard. I suppose he'd wanted a wife to help with the work. Or maybe he thought marrying a young woman would let him get hard again. It didn't. He tried at first, but he couldn't get it hard enough to go in.

"He would play with it with his hand and that would get it up just a little. But by the time he got on top of me it was always soft again. That made him mad and . . . two or three times he hit me after. I guess he decided it was my fault if I wasn't woman enough or pretty enough or young enough to make him able to perform again.

"Then after a time he quit trying. Quit hitting me too, thank goodness. We didn't sleep together after he quit trying to break my cherry." She shrugged. "And then he died. Crazy, isn't it? A widow who runs a whorehouse and she's a virgin. Who would've thought it."

"I didn't know," Dex said.

"No, of course you wouldn't."

He took her into his arms and kissed her again. "Thank you. It's a wonderful gift you've given me. I am honored that it was me you allowed this first time. Any regrets now?"

Ellie smiled and shook her head. "No. No regrets, Dexter. I just hope . . ." She giggled. "I'll have to ask one of my girls about how to keep from getting pregnant. They know all about that sort of thing."

"That's a good idea." Dex considered it a major blessing that it was women who had to worry about that stuff. The gentleman need concern himself only with the fun. It was only the woman who risked public censure if the unexpected and unwanted did occur.

"What time is it?"

Dex rolled over to look at the key-wind clock that squatted on top of Ellie's tall chest of drawers. "Half past three."

"Do you think she's been enjoying her bath in the coffee long enough now?"

He grinned. "Let's go take a look."

• 42 •

"What should we call her?"

"Princess," Ellie said without having to pause for thought. Dex suspected the thought of a name was not a new one to Ellie. But then Ellie was the creator of this really quite beautiful little figure. Dex only came up with the idea. Ellie was the sculptor.

"Then Princess it shall be," Dex said. "But only between ourselves."

"Yes. Only between us two." She stood peering into the coffee-filled tub with one arm around Dex's waist, as if she did not want to lose fleshly contact with him quite yet. She gave a little hug now, then let go of him and dropped to her knees beside the tub.

"She really is beautiful," Dex told her. "I could almost believe it myself if I didn't know better."

"Thank you. I think we can take her out now, don't you?"

"Sure. Lay the sheet out. On that chair would be good, I think."

"Be careful with her." Ellie went to fold the sheet and spread it over the side-by-side seats of two chairs that she dragged close together. Hers was a better idea, he saw. It would give more support to the carved limestone figurine.

When the padding was ready, Dex bent and with considerable effort lifted the figure free, cold coffee dripping onto the rag rug as he carried Princess to her temporary bed.

"It's going to be a damned shame to rub dirt all over her," he said.

"We have to do it though. She's supposed to have been buried out there for, what would you say? A thousand years?"

"Oh, four or five thousand at least," Dex said.

"No more than four," Ellie corrected him.

"Pardon me?"

"Scholars have worked out from reading the Bible that the earth can't be more than four thousand and some years old. I forget exactly how old they say it is." She smiled. "I have a circuit preacher as a regular client. He's told me all about these theories."

"How do they explain things like those dinosaur bones they've found in Wyoming? Or the fossilized fish and things found in rocks?"

Ellie shrugged. "I didn't ask."

"Not that I'm going to argue with them. Four thousand is old enough for me."

"She is pretty, isn't she?"

The figure Ellie had carved was slightly less than three feet tall, a size dictated by the chunk of limestone Dex had been able to find and sneak into the house. She was deliberately made with lines that were not quite sharp. But then she was supposed to be an accretion of lime built up over millennia—however many of them one wished to assume— to replace original bone and flesh. Despite that, Ellie's work really was quite lovely.

It was the replication of a tiny woman, her arms by her sides, nose straight and lips thin, one eye partially open and its socket empty—Dex had thought that a nice touch—with elongated ears, the overlarge lobes giving her a distinctly foreign appearance. Not quite the same as humans were nowadays.

Her limestone hair had been pulled tight against her

scalp. Her nipples were small—as were Ellie's, Dex so recently discovered—and her legs lay just enough apart that there was a hint of pudendum showing in a hairless crotch. When she carved that Dex had worried that the figure might be mistaken for a child's, but by the time he said anything Ellie had already chiseled away the stone that would have been required to make a furry snatch.

One foot was small and delicate. The other was missing, the appearance being that it must have been broken off in the process of recovery.

Scientists would someday be welcome to dig for the missing foot themselves if they wished.

The real reason there was no right foot, however, was that the limestone block had been too narrow to permit the carving of both. So Ellie came up with the idea of having one foot gone as a solution.

"What do you think, Dexter?"

He laughed. "I think that if some charlatan back East can have his Cardiff Giant, ma'am, then we are equally entitled to our Winter Grove Pixie."

Ellie laughed with him, then—obviously happy with her work, with Dexter, perhaps even with herself now—began mopping pockets of coffee off the dark tan surfaces of Princess, the Winter Grove Pixie.

• 43 •

"Don't go," Ellie said, wrapping her arms tight around him and nuzzling his neck.

"I have to," he told her.

"But you'll be back tonight, won't you?" She nibbled his ear. Ellie had gotten a late start, but she was a quick learner. Dex could feel a stirring of renewed interest.

"Matter of fact," he said, "I won't be. I need to ride over to Connor and get those telegrams off."

"Do you have to do it today?"

"Yes."

"But you don't have to leave right now," she persisted.

"Mmm . . . no." He smiled. And kissed her. "I expect maybe I don't, at that."

Ellie licked and kissed her way from one side of his neck to the other, gave full and careful attention to his chest and then further down until she reached his cock.

She hadn't said anything about it exactly, but Dex had gotten the impression that probably her late husband tried to get her to work up an erection for him in her mouth. She probably resented that as a requirement. Now she spent several long minutes examining his pecker. Looking it over at close-up range. Sniffing it—which couldn't have been much of a thrill, considering how often and how thoroughly it had been used through the past night—touching it very tentatively with her tongue and finally, finally taking it into her mouth.

By the time she got around to that, Dex was as hard and randy as a fifteen-year-old boy with a tit in his hand for the first time in his life.

No, he thought firmly, he really did not have to dress and leave at this very minute.

Dex did not have to ask how to find the telegraph office in the county seat. He simply followed the wire and poles from the flat north of town and came to the end of both at a mercantile on the east side of the business district.

"How can I help you, sir?"

"I have a wire to get off."

"That's what I'm here for."

"I'll want to send only the one message, but I want it sent to a rather long list of recipients."

"That's no problem, sir."

"And in the addressing process, will each recipient see who the others are?" he asked.

"Not if you don't want them to, sir."

Dex smiled. "And . . . if I *do* want everyone to see the full list?"

"That can be arranged too, sir."

Dex pulled an envelope from inside his coat and laid it on the counter. "The message is here. So is the list of addresses. I, uh, I would prefer that the recipients know that others have been told, that there will be competition, so to speak. But I don't want to tell them that in so many words, if you take my meaning."

"I will be glad to see to that, sir."

"In that case, please work up the cost of the telegrams." Dex winked at the fellow. "And add a twenty-dollar tip for your troubles if you please."

"*Thank you*, sir. Thank you very much." The telegrapher was quick to open the envelope and get busy once he had that little extra added instruction.

Dex paid for the service in gold coin, thanked the man and headed for the saloon where he'd found wee Amanda the last time he was in town.

Everything considered, the tiny whore was owed a debt of thanks for her unintended inspiration for Princess, and Dex always liked to pay his debts.

Besides, he thought with relish, he would have to sleep somewhere tonight. He might as well be comfortable doing it.

He was already anticipating with considerable pleasure the plan he had for tomorrow morning. He was eager to see the look on Amanda's face when he handed her a fifty-dollar tip on top of her usual fee for services.

· 44 ·

Dex was back in Winter Grove in time for lunch but he didn't even consider stopping in town and waiting until evening. He rode straight on out to the whorehouse without so much as dismounting in town.

It was long before working hours but there was a driving rig parked beside the place. Dex left his horse at one of the hitching rails and approached the door. He could hear a commotion going on inside. Not shouting exactly. It didn't sound quite like anything he'd heard before. But whatever it was he didn't like it. He tried the knob and, finding the door unlocked, went in without knocking.

There was a commotion, all right. C. Julian Blake was there. And a friend. Blake had the Mexican, knife fancier Luis with him. The little SOB must have replaced Joshua Bonner as Blake's bodyguard and errand boy, Dex guessed. Must've been keeping well out of sight too or Marshal Harris would have arrested the little bastard for trying to skewer Dex that day in the livery stable.

None of that mattered right at this moment though. Blake, his face and jaw a huge, white blob of linen bandage wrappings and oddly shaped wooden splints, was trying to scream curses and threats at Ellie. He was considerably hampered in that effort by the fact that he couldn't open his mouth to shout with. His attempts at imprecation came out more like angry, keening growls. Specific words could be deduced if one wanted to bother, but they were slurred largely beyond recognition by the man's physical limitations of the moment.

Blake blustered and bellowed, but it was Luis that Dex was worried about. The little pigsticker was standing too close to Ellie for Dex's comfort.

Dex slammed the door loudly as a means to announce his arrival.

He smiled when all three faces turned to see who it was who'd barged in on them uninvited. "Afternoon, folks," Dex said calmly. "Nice to see you all. Come by to make an ass of yourself again, Curtis? Be a nice boy or I'll jump up and down on your face again." Dex's smile became all the wider and he feigned an angelic innocence of expression. "We could see if we can't immobilize that jaw permanently if you like, Curtis."

Blake grunted something that Dex could not begin to understand, but Luis did. The Mexican left Ellie's side— that was an improvement, Dex thought—and marched closer to face Dex. "There is still a price on your head," he snapped.

"Yes, and if you were man enough to collect it I expect I'd have to worry about that, wouldn't I?" Dex returned.

Luis flushed a dark red beneath the brown of his complexion. "You don' have your big knife today, señor."

The little man was about half right. Dex had left it on his saddle. "You want me to go get it? I seem to remember you running like a jackass rabbit the last time you got a look at my blade."

"I could kill you, señor. I think prob'ly I will."

"Anytime it pleases you to try, Luis," Dex invited. He laid a hand on the grips of the big Webley on his belt and smiled like an indulgent uncle waiting to see a child show off some new parlor trick.

Not surprisingly, Luis did not appear to find this a good time. He held himself stiff and as tall as he was able to manage, and he twitched his shoulders as he puffed himself up like a scrawny fighting rooster. But he did not reach for his knife, and after a few seconds of preening and posturing he backed down and went to stand beside his boss.

"Are these people bothering you, Ellie?" Dex asked.

"Yes." She winked at him. "It seems that Curtis has heard, shall we say, rumors."

Dex laughed. "That was quick. I thought it would take another day or two." He gave the lawyer a mocking bow. "Let me commend you, Mr. Blake. Your resources are good."

"You thought I wouldn't know. That's why you went to Connor. To hide what you did." At least that was what Dex *thought* Blake said. The man's diction being what it was through locked teeth it was also possible that he'd just recited a recipe for rhubarb pie.

"He was also asking why I've ordered a glass-top display case from a carpenter in town," Ellie said. "And who would be paying for it. He thinks I've been holding money out on him."

Blake looked nervously from Ellie to Dex and back again. The worry in his eyes—he didn't have enough face visible to be sure of his expressions, actually—reminded Dex that no one was supposed to know that Ellie's purported ownership of the whorehouse was only a false front to shield Blake's reputation.

If it hadn't been that Dex wanted the son of a bitch's cooperation in freeing James he probably would have settled for damaging the man by exposing him.

That, however, was not the object of all this. Getting James out of jail was. And being able to yank Ellie Adams out from under his control had become a part of the goal too now. Neither of those could be accomplished by anything as simple as an attack on the bastard's character. Well, sort of "character." Dex wasn't entirely sure Blake deserved the term for his true self. In any event, what they needed was to force Blake into a position that would gain what they wanted. Exposing him to public censure would be pleasant if it were to happen, but that would be entirely secondary to the primary purpose here.

"I loaned Mrs. Adams the money for the box," Dex said. "And don't bother asking about the price of the telegraph messages. I paid for those too."

Blake sounded like he was gargling with salt water. Dex took that to be a question and more than likely the most obvious question.

"Because I like her," Dex said.

Blake gurgled and sputtered and spewed out incomprehensible sounds. Dex tried to figure them out. He really did. But none of it made any sense to him. After a minute or so he held his hand up in an attempt to stop the flow and shrugged his shoulders to indicate that he just wasn't getting any of it.

Blake seemed more frustrated than ever. He tried turning to Luis to act as an interpreter, but while Luis was probably capable of translating English to Spanish, this was beyond his linguistic abilities. The would-be assassin could do nothing with the flow of Curtis Blake's guttural babble. He too gave up with a shrug.

Blake uttered one final comment. Even without being able to understand it, Dex felt reasonably sure it was a word that a gentleman should not utter in the presence of a lady.

With that the lawyer turned and stalked out, Luis trailing behind. The knife man slowed long enough to give Dex a withering glare—Dex failed to wither on command, but that was not Luis's fault—then had the good manners to very carefully close and latch the door behind him.

Ellie looked at Dex and began to clap her hands with considerable glee.

"It's working," she declared. "Just like you said it would, Dexter. It's working already."

Dex opened his arms, and Ellie hurried into them.

· 45 ·

They placed the display case in the old Adams homestead instead of the whorehouse.

"Blake could make a pretty sound argument that he owns the house and has the right to see anything that's in it," Dex had explained when Ellie made a sour face at his mention of the soddy. "I don't think he would want to expose his interest in the place, but he could always claim he built it for your use because you and he were having a love affair or some such lie. He could even try to damage you by claiming you started the affair when your husband was still alive. I wouldn't put much of anything past that man. It will be a whole lot safer to use the old place. Good grief, he might even claim ownership of Princess on the basis of it being on his property. And you know Grassley would rule however Blake wanted him to. I really think we're safer putting her out there. Besides, we already have a guard on duty there."

"All right. If you say so."

"I'm afraid so."

So they put the case and Princess in Ellie's cabriolet—also courtesy of Curtis Blake's unfailing generosity—and drove out back to the soddy.

Joshua climbed down from his rooftop perch to meet them in the yard.

"Did you bring those shells I asked for?" he asked first off. "I've about shot up the last batch."

"I brought them. Two cases this time," Dex said, "and if that doesn't hold you for a few days I'll have to buy you some new guns too. You're apt to wear these out before the end of the week."

Joshua looked as pleased as if he'd been given a new toy.

Joshua bobbed his head and touched the brim of his hat respectfully, then helped Ellie down from the buggy and went onto tiptoe to peer inside. Dex couldn't decide if he was looking at the carefully padded bundle they'd brought or if he was merely anxious to get his hands on the cases of .45 cartridges Dex brought for his target practice.

That was one thing Dex had learned about Joshua. He seemed incapable of taking a simple interest in something. Whatever it was that caught his fancy, he was obsessed by it.

"Help me take this thing inside," Dex said.

"This the thing I'm supposed to guard?" Joshua asked.

"Sure is. This, the digging site, it's all important. You'll see."

They carried the display case in first. The carpenter had built it to the exact specifications Dex provided. The box was essentially a coffin, large enough to hold a normal human being—Dex thought the reminder of scale would be a nice touch when people viewed the "remains" of Princess inside it—but with a glass top. The work had been done with skill and care, the raw wood smoothed and stained and polished.

A puffy bed of ruby red satin pillows was provided. Dex wasn't sure about the choice of red, but that was what was on hand in the whorehouse and he couldn't see any point in ordering some other color pillow and waiting for them to be shipped in from a distant city. The red would simply have to do.

Ellie directed the positioning of the case inside the small

soddy. She only made them shift it here and yon five or six times before she was satisfied with where it sat.

"Are you ready for this?" Dex asked.

Joshua shrugged. Furniture and things like that were not on his list of interests to obsess about. He followed Dex out to the cabriolet and grabbed for Princess in her thick wrappings.

Dex shuddered at the possibility that Joshua might drop the precious object and destroy their plan with it. "You get your cartridges, Joshua. I'll take our archeological find."

"Your what?"

"I'll show you when we get it inside."

That suited Joshua just fine. He picked up his cases of .45s and Dex took Princess in with tender care.

Ellie held the glass open and helped with the unwrapping.

"Jesus," Joshua blurted. "Is that a body or something?"

"Something like that," Dex told him.

"A dead kid?"

"We don't think so. She's full grown. Take a look." Dex knew good and well it was the tits and pussy Joshua would be staring at. It was no accident that Ellie carved those details with such care.

"Jeez, she sure as hell is." Joshua gave Ellie a stricken look and hastened to apologize for his language.

"That's all right, Joshua. It amazed us too," Ellie said.

"You know that half-dug well you've been guarding?" Dex asked. "Well this right here is the reason why. Mrs. Adams hired a man to dig a well, but he struck this before he got down to water. She could be . . . we don't know yet, of course . . . but she could be thousands of years old. You can see how she's been calcified over time."

"Yeah, I sure can."

Dex was as certain as sin that Joshua had no idea what the word calcified meant. But he nodded as sage as an owl and agreed that, yep, this body was calcified sure enough.

"Is this what you call a mummy?" Joshua asked.

"Not exactly. But it's sort of like that. Terribly, terribly old anyway. And who knows, there could be more just like

this buried in the ground out here. Now do you see why
we've wanted this place guarded?"

"I sure do." Joshua kept staring at Princess while he
spoke. He seemed very much in awe of her.

But then that was precisely the idea.

Dex was hoping Princess would awe 'em all, from ocean
to ocean. Hell, from continent to continent. Why not? After
all, his telegrams had gone out to half the major newspapers
in the United States and its territories. By now there should
be reporters, scientists too for all he knew, headed for Winter Grove in herds and hordes and bunches.

Why, he really should have bought stock in the railroad
before the announcements were made. With all the increase
in traffic coming this way their revenues were bound to go
up.

Ellie made a few tiny adjustments to the way the pillows
lay around Princess—they wanted her to look as comfortable as a 4,000-year-old dead woman can manage—then
closed the glass lid.

The carpenter had been instructed to provide for the display case to be secured with multiple locks. Dex did the
honors and handed the keys to Ellie.

"There will be lots of people coming out here very soon,"
he warned Joshua. "Your job is to make sure none of them
comes near this, uh, calcified body. Not until or unless either Mrs. Adams or I am accompanying them."

Joshua bobbed his head.

"We're counting on you, Josh. This is important."

"I won't let you down, Dexter. Miz Adams, ma'am.
That's a promise."

"Good man, Joshua. Thanks."

· 46 ·

Cause a stir? Dex damned well intended to. But even he
hadn't figured the half of it.

Within a week of sending the telegrams, Winter Grove
was practically awash with travelers. There were eight new-
comers, actually. For Winter Grove that was awash and
then some.

The half-assed hotel in town had only six rooms. And
the price of those doubled on the first day, then doubled
again by the third. When the owner decided that guests
would have to share the rooms—and beds—Dex decided
not to fight the inflation. He said the hell with that nonsense
and moved out to the whorehouse with Ellie.

Curtis Blake was furious. But then he was probably one
of the few in Winter Grove who appreciated what celebrity
like this could lead to.

Big money, that's what it could lead to.

But none of that would be going into his pockets.

No, Dex realized, that was not entirely accurate. A little
of the tourist income would certainly trickle into Blake's
pockets, if only because a good many of the newspapermen
who made up the first wave of visitors would be wanting

to enjoy the services of the young ladies—so to speak—at
the whorehouse.

But the big money that would start rolling in as soon as
the news flashed around the world would come in the form
of admission fees for a look inside that glass-top display
case.

As it was even the newspaper reporters were required to
pay. And since they would profit from the story themselves
and be reimbursed for expenses by their newspapers, Dex
and Ellie set their viewing fees at ten dollars.

It was an outrageous price, of course. Hell yes, it was.
But the newspapers could afford it, and anyway Dex was
very well aware that you make something more valuable
by setting a high value on it.

The worse he and Ellie gouged the newsmen the more
likely they were to accept this wild tale of a Winter Grove
Pixie as the genuine article.

Some of them, after all, might be old enough to remember the widespread excitement when the Cardiff Giant was
"discovered" and make a connection between these two
rather remarkable finds.

Dex believed that would be less likely if Ellie showed
full confidence in her Princess.

Joshua Bonner was so busy guarding a bit of slightly
modified limestone and collecting fees for entry to the sanctum sanctum where the fraud was housed that he had little
time to continue his target practice.

Dex mollified him somewhat by doubling Joshua's salary
and giving him the job title of chief of security.

Not that there was any formal organization to be the chief
of. But then why quibble about mere technicalities. Joshua
was proud of both the raise and the title.

"Dexter," Joshua asked on one of Dex's frequent visits
to the soddy, "this man says he should get in free today
because he paid his ten dollars yesterday." He pointed to a
skinny fellow in a tweed suit and spectacles. The reporter
looked like he wasn't yet old enough to shave, but he had
a notepad in hand and a collection of pencils peeking out
of his breast pocket.

"Was he here yesterday?"

"Yes, he surely was. I remember him. He's telling the truth."

"Good," Dex said. "It's always a pleasure to meet an honest man." He smiled. "They're very rare, you know." His smile got bigger. He did, after all, know what he was talking about in that regard. Rarer, in fact, than any of these reporters suspected. "But I'm afraid yesterday's entry fee was for yesterday only. If you want to see the Pixie again today you have to pay again."

The poor fellow looked so crestfallen that Dex wondered if he was not a staff writer at all but had to pay his own expenses if he wanted this breaking news story.

"Could I ask you, sir, if you could, um, tell me anything about the discovery? Were you here at the time?"

"I was," Dex said modestly. "I was here discussing something with the prisoner who was digging the well for Mrs. Adams."

"Yes, sir. Do you happen to know the prisoner's name?"

"I do, but I think it would only be fair for you to discuss that with Marshal Harris. I don't know what his policies might be about that, and I wouldn't want to do anything in violation of his rules."

"Yes sir, thank you. But may I take it that you did see the, um, pixie's, uh, body while it was still in the ground?"

"That's right."

"And you recognized it immediately for what it was?"

"No, I did not. In fact, I'm not at all sure even now just who or what this find represents. My first thought was that we'd stumbled across a buried child. But when we got a closer look that was obviously not the case. As I believe you may already have noticed."

"Yes, I have." The young reporter blushed. A bright, cherry red flush developed in the vicinity of his ears and spread across his cheeks and down his neck. A virgin, Dex guessed. Maybe never saw a naked female before. No wonder he wanted to go in and look again.

"Exactly," Dex said. "And someone . . . it might have been Mrs. Adams, but then she would not have been looking quite so intently at certain other portions of the, um, anatomy, don't you see . . . in any event I believe it was she who noticed the shape of the figure's ears. They do not look quite human, do they?"

"I . . . I didn't notice that, sir."

"Really? You should remember to look at them next time. Those are what really suggest to me that this figure is not that of a dead human woman. At least not any sort of being that we today would recognize as human."

"How do you explain the mummy being here, sir?"

"Frankly, I have no explanations to offer. That would be for scientists to explain, and I certainly could not qualify in that regard. I do know from my own college schooling, however, that this figure is not mummified. Rather it is very probably a calcified object. That is, it is not a true body. There are no tissues present, and the thing you see here never walked the earth or breathed the air." And that was a truthful statement at last, by gum.

"What I believe happened . . . and again I hasten to add that it will take scientific analysis before anyone will really know . . . but what I believe happened is that a person who looked exactly like this figure lived and somehow died. Whether her people buried her or she was covered over through happenstance, I cannot speculate. Somehow, though, while she was in the ground for," he shrugged, "however many years, thousands perhaps, somehow during this time the tissues of her physical body were dissolved and slowly replaced with minerals native to the soil. I remember reading a little about this process when I was in school, but of course I am not an expert. I offer only guess-work. It will take scientists to give us real explanations."

It would take a real scientist a good, oh, ten or fifteen seconds to spot the hoax, Dex guessed.

Or not. He understood that even some scientists accepted the Giant as a legitimate find. It wasn't until some years after the "discovery" that a sharper eye disclosed the truth.

"Will the pixie be placed on display for the public, sir?" the reporter asked.

"That, of course, will be a decision made by Mrs. Adams. The land, after all, is hers to do with as she pleases. But if I may tell you in confidence," confidence his rosy red ass, Dex thought; the reporter was so eager for details that he looked like a bird dog on point, "it is my understanding that Mrs. Adams plans to erect a hotel and restaurant combination on this site and to create a tourist destination and resort with the Winter Grove Pixie as its focus."

That last bit Dex thought of only on the spur of the moment. But he liked it. And intended to expand on it in other interviews that were sure to follow. He'd have to remember to fill Ellie in about it too so she would tell the same story.

After all, the more of the pie that was likely to fall into Ellie's lap, the more eager Curtis Blake would be to snatch that away from her and into his own pocket.

But yeah, a hotel and restaurant out here sounded like a splendid idea.

It was bound to piss Blake off.

Dex had a little trouble keeping a smile off his face while the young reporter remained close by.

"You said something about the ears, sir?"

"That's right. They don't look quite human to me."

The young man hesitated in thought. Then dug into his pockets in search of a ten-dollar eagle to put into Joshua's waiting palm. "I think I should look at her one more time, don't you?" he asked of neither of them in particular.

"I really think you should," Dex agreed.

Hell, just off the reporters who were continuing to stream into Winter Grove now at the rate of three or four a day, Ellie was going to come out with a profit.

But then the real return on the investment was yet to come. The bait had been placed. Now Dex only needed to wait for C. Julian Blake to come to the scent. To the scent of money.

Dex was smiling quite happily when he remounted and rode back to the house where Ellie should be waiting, ready for a little afternoon amusement. Now that the girl had learned what that particular portion of her anatomy was good for she was damn near insatiable.

He was *not* complaining.

• 47 •

Within two weeks the town of Winter Grove was inundated with tourists who were streaming in from the more accessible cities like Denver, Kansas City and St. Louis.

And Dex was very well aware that this was only the first wave of visitors. Others who had to come from greater distances were already on the way. They'd had telegraphic requests for information and for reservations—not that there was anything to reserve, but the distant parties did not yet know that—from New York and Boston, San Francisco and Seattle.

It wasn't even stopping there. A team of scientists from the University of Edinburgh sent a cable begging Ellie to allow them first rights of inspection, as did a Count something-or-other from Poland and an amateur fossil hunter from Norway who had a worldwide reputation. Cable and telegraph messages had similarly arrived from parties in Ascuncion, Macao, Stockholm, London and St. Petersburg, Russia.

This thing was taking on such a complete life of its own that Dex was afraid it might somehow backfire.

Not that he was willing to back off. Not hardly. His philosophy was: When in doubt, turn up the wick.

He hired two assistants for Joshua to supervise—which pleased the chief of security to no end—paying for them out of the revenues brought in from entry and viewing fees.

Now that the first flush of excitement was past and most of the reporters had already left, the viewing fee was reduced to fifty cents for a brief, pass-through look at Princess. And even so the money continued to roll in very nicely. Dex's investment in the scam had already been repaid, and Ellie insisted that he accept a fifty-percent share of the profits.

Dex was a gentleman of the old style. He was also an eminently practical fellow. He gave Ellie a big kiss—and certain other expressions of gratitude as well—and accepted the money without demur.

Modesty and self-deprecation can, after all, be taken to unseemly extremes.

His latest idea was to lay out a foundation outline for the hotel and restaurant combination both he and Ellie had touted to the reporters. He had no intention whatsoever of laying out the cash to actually build such a resort. But it wouldn't hurt to make Curtis Blake think that he was.

With Joshua's help, Dex spent the afternoon cheerfully pounding stakes into the hard, sunbaked soil and stringing twine from one stake to another.

Once he was in the spirit of the thing he rather enjoyed himself, determining there should be a dining room here, a gentleman's spa there, mud baths and massage tables for the ladies over there. He hummed softly to himself while he pounded and pulled and in the recesses of his mind visualized things that would never be.

"D'you have everything under control here, Joshua?"

"You can count on me, Dexter."

"I know I can, Joshua."

"Want to take today's money poke back with you now?" Joshua asked.

Dex glanced down the old path toward town, recent use having turned it into a very well-marked road. He could see two light coaches rolling out to the Princess site, each of them trailing a plume of yellow dust. It amazed him how quickly someone in Connor had been able to secure worn-out army ambulances and put them into service as a link between Princess and the nearest railroad.

"No," Dex told his chief of security, "you have more viewers coming. No point in having to count money twice. Just bring the bag over to the house after you've closed up for the night like usual."

"I'll see you then, Dexter."

Dex gave Joshua a smile and touched the brim of his hat in salute, then mounted his horse and headed back to the whorehouse at an easy lope.

• 48 •

Well, well, well, Dex thought as he came near the house. That certainly did look like Curtis Blake's carriage parked on the far side of the place. Dex involuntarily touched the butt of the big Webley to reassure himself that it was there. Wherever Blake was these days, Luis was sure to be also.

Dex dismounted and tied his horse, then fetched his cane from the saddle scabbard that was originally intended to hold a carbine but which served equally well for carrying a sword cane. When Luis was around Dex wanted to make it clear that he still had the longer knife. And a will to use it that was every bit as strong as Luis did.

"Miz Ellie say if you come home d'you please join her in her office," Betty Lou greeted him. Dex relinquished his hat to the servant but kept the cane. "Thank you, Betty Lou."

"Yes sir."

Betty Lou went upstairs. Dex took the now very familiar route through the piano room and on to the back of the place. He let himself into Ellie's office without knocking.

Ellie was seated behind her desk. Blake was standing in front of it. Luis was beside and half a step back of Blake, a dog come perfectly to heel. The knife fighter gave Dex an evil glare but made no overt threats.

"Dexter, dear. Did you get the hotel laid out to your liking?" Ellie greeted him.

"I think you'll like it," Dex said. "We should be able to accommodate twenty guests at a time. Or do you think we should expand that?" He smiled. "We can discuss that later, I suppose."

Blake glowered. He still had to wear his wood-and-linen splints, Dex saw, but much of the swelling seemed to have gone down. "You people have no right . . ." He was speaking better too. His words were still slurred but at least Dex had no difficulty understanding what the man was trying to say now.

"On the contrary," Dex said in a mild voice. "Mrs. Adams has every right. In fact . . . we hadn't planned on telling you this right away," largely because he'd only thought of it just now, "but we've been thinking of closing this, um, establishment. It doesn't fit in with the image we want to project to the world." He smiled, his expression bland. If that didn't turn up the wick on Blake, he didn't know what in hell would.

Ellie received the news with no change of expression although it was as new to her as it was to Blake. "That's right, Curtis. I am sure you understand."

"Damn you! Both of you." Blake acted like he intended to raise his hand.

"Careful, Curtis. Make any sort of threatening gesture toward Mrs. Adams and I'll undo all the good healing you've done since the last time I rearranged your face." He looked at Luis. "And there wouldn't be a thing you could do to stop me, little man."

Luis looked like he was ready to go to the daggers. Except of course it wasn't a dagger but a sword that Dex would be using, and there was no way even a very good man with a knife can oppose a man who knows what he was doing with his sword. Dex knew what he was doing with the sword. Luis went pale with fury and trembled from the effort of containing his rage. But he managed. He remained as still and silent as a coiled snake.

In this case, though, Dex had every confidence that he was the true danger. When it came to coiling to strike, Luis was second rate.

Curtis Blake turned a bright and vivid shade of red. His mouth gaped like a fish sucking thin air, and he too was atremble. He looked ready to explode, but like Luis he managed to contain his impulses. After a few moments in which to adjust to this news, he said, "This is my property."

"Of course it is," Ellie said agreeably. "Would you like it back? You're welcome to dismantle it and take it wherever you wish, Curtis. Of course in that case everyone in the county will know that you are the real owner." She smiled.

"And the real whoremonger. What public office was it that you had your hopes pinned to, Curtis? The governorship, was it?" Her smile had the same sparkle as a flake of cut glass posing as a diamond.

"You can't do that," Blake blustered. "We have an agreement."

"Yes, we do. And I've lived up to every aspect of it. Now I am terminating the agreement. The girls are your employees, Curtis. You can take them with you when you leave."

"But I can't . . . where would I . . . you can't possibly mean . . ."

Ellie only continued to look at him. And to smile that huge, beatific, quite thoroughly phony smile. Now that Dex had proposed the idea that she get out of the whorehouse management business she seemed entirely satisfied with the prospect.

◆ 49 ◆

Dex wanted to offer the suggestion so bad he could scarcely contain himself. But he didn't dare do that, and he knew it. If he or Ellie came up with the idea that Blake buy her out it could raise suspicions. It had to be his own idea or it wouldn't likely work.

Finally the obtuse son of a bitch figured it out. "Let's be reasonable about this," Blake said. "Of course I have an interest in high office. I've never tried to hide that. But I need a financial base to build on. Nothing wrong with that, is there? Of course not. So let's see if we can't work out some way to, um, accommodate your needs and mine alike."

"I don't know about you, Curtis, but I am out of the business of whoring. As of this afternoon. And I will remind you that your building sits on my land. Like I said before, you are welcome to do whatever you like with it. It's yours. But do not expect me to dance to your tune any longer."

"You owe a considerable amount of money, may I remind you?"

Ellie smiled. "I am now capable of paying off a considerable amount." Her expression only seemed to be a smile.

In truth it was a taunt. And Curtis Blake could see that full well.

Blake sputtered and fumed a little. Dex suspected he was merely buying time, trying to think this through.

Hopefully of course he would arrive at the point where Dex and Ellie wanted him to be.

And so he was.

"Look," Blake said in his best imitation of sincerity and sweet reason, "we've always gotten on very well, Ellie. You and I together have prospered. But now you have opportunity before you. What would you say to the idea that we dissolve our, um, partnership and that I, well, that I buy out your position. I would, of course, wipe off the debt. And I could offer you a, shall we say, substantial amount for your land and, uh, whatever the property may contain."

"The Pixie and all tourism revenues deriving from it, you mean," Ellie said.

"Exactly," Blake said.

Ellie pursed her lips. Steepled her fingertips beneath her chin. Swiveled her chair around so she faced the wall, only the back of her head visible above the seat back.

Good girl, Dex was thinking. Don't make it too easy for him. Don't do anything to make the SOB suspicious.

Eventually Ellie turned around to face the room again. "What exactly do you have in mind, Curtis?"

He beamed.

Dex always liked it when a sheep proposed the terms of its own shearing. Yessir, he surely did.

With Luis and Dexter looking silently on, Ellie and Blake began the process of negotiating the price Blake would pay for the privilege of making a fool of himself.

· 50 ·

Dex drove the short distance into town three days later with Ellie at his side. It had all been worked out, with enough cash paid in hand that Ellie could return home to the softer, gentler climate of the South with money enough to establish a genteel if not entirely luxurious life for herself.

Now only one detail remained and that was the stipulation—Ellie had demanded it and would not budge from her negotiating position about it—that Judge Grassley void the order placing James in jail. As soon as James was released, Ellie would affix her signature to the final documents transferring ownership of the Ned Adams farm to C. Julian Blake.

Easy as the proverbial candy-from-a-baby. All over and done with now.

So why was it, Dex asked himself, that he was still nervous.

He would be damn-all glad to put Winter Grove behind them. He'd enjoyed Ellie's company here well enough, but she would be leaving in a matter of days anyway. Just as soon as James was freed, Dex wanted to be on horseback again and making tracks for parts unknown.

For one thing, he wanted to put Luis and that knife well behind them. After all, Luis knew about Jane Carter's reward offer for Dex's head. And why place temptation in the poor fellow's way, eh?

No, Dex would most definitely feel better once this town was behind them. Miles and miles behind.

They rolled to a halt in front of Marshal Harris's jail and were met there by his deputy Henry Langley.

"Marshal said I should tell you that the judge is holding hearings today in the church building," Langley said.

"In the church? Really?"

Langley shrugged. "It's the only place big enough for trials and stuff. Except the saloon. And Dan over at the saloon doesn't want to shut down his bar and lose all that business now there's so many folks in town."

Dex chuckled. The tourist trade was running strong. But Ellie's timing for getting out of the pixie business was impeccable. Curtis Blake didn't know it, but the first contingent of scientists was due later this week. Ellie received the message announcing their travel plans just the day before.

Now, of course, the scientists and whatever they discovered about Princess would be Blake's affair. Or his problem. Whatever. Dex's smile was positively wicked as he followed the sight of the church steeple out to the edge of town and dropped the hitch weight before he helped Ellie out of the cabriolet.

"Looks like we won't be alone," he observed. Blake's carriage was already there, as were several horses.

Joshua Bonner met them on the front steps of the little church. "What are you doing here, Joshua?"

Bonner grinned. "Wanted to say good-bye," he said.

"You're leaving?"

Joshua nodded. "Mr. Blake fired me again. But I've put a lot of money by with what you paid me. I think I'm gonna go to Denver and, I dunno, buy me a business maybe. If you ever come to Denver, Dexter, you look me up."

"I'll do that too," Dex said.

Joshua followed them to the door of the church but did

not go inside with them. Could be that piety made him nervous, Dex thought.

Marshal Harris met them just inside. "You'll have to leave your guns and that sword here in the vestibule," he said. "Apart from this being a church it's also a court of law today. We have to follow the rules, you know."

"Blake and his man have had to do the same?" Dex asked.

"I took their guns myself," the marshal said, "and three knives from that Mexican fellow."

"All right then. I expect I can do the same." Dex gave up both his Webleys and the sword cane.

"Go ahead," Harris said, motioning them forward.

Herbert Grassley was seated behind a draped table that no doubt served as an altar on other occasions.

James, without handcuffs or leg irons now that he was about to be released from custody, was sitting in a pew on the right side of the church. Blake and Luis were in the front pew on the left.

The proceeding took practically no time. Blake asked permission to speak. Grassley granted it. Blake withdrew his charge against James, and Grassley whacked the church altar with a gavel while he solemnly proclaimed that the prisoner should be released.

James looked as relieved now as Dex felt. The two friends shook hands and spent the first few moments of James's newfound freedom just looking at each other and grinning. After a minute or two Dex said, "Your things are all out at Ellie's place."

"You must be Mrs. Adams," James said.

Ellie pretended not to have heard and acted like she didn't see James. But then she was a Southern gentlelady of breeding and, now, independence. Of course she would not acknowledge social pleasantries from a Negro. The knowledge peeved Dex a little although James seemed to accept it as a matter of course.

"We'll have lunch on the trail," Dex said. "I want this place behind us."

"Couldn't be too soon to suit me," James told him.

James trailed by several steps as Dex took Ellie's arm and led her toward the church doors.

"Aren't you forgetting something?" Blake asked. "I have paper for you to sign now. That was the last detail I believe."

"Of course. Excuse me, Dexter?"

Dex and James ambled on, out onto the front steps.

Luis followed.

It occurred to Dex as they stepped into the sunshine that the guns and sword cane he'd left in the church vestibule were not in evidence now. Nor, come to think of it, had James's guns been returned to him.

Marshal Harris was still inside.

And Luis was standing between Dex and the people who remained inside the church.

· 51 ·

"That woman in Texas," Luis said. "She don't care if your head is still with the rest of you when she gets it. You know?"

"You'll play hell trying to take it without those knives of yours," Dex told him.

"You'd have to fight the both of us," James put in. "I doubt you'd want to do that."

"Fight you? Why the hell I do a thing like that, eh? I think I just shoot the both of you. Then I put that head in a pickle jar an' take it to the lady."

"Bull," Dex said. "Marshal Harris took your knives. Guns too if you had any."

Luis laughed. "He tol' you that, did he?"

"So he did, yes."

Luis laughed again. And pulled his coat back to expose a pair of revolvers that looked remarkably like James's guns.

"Shit," Dex said.

"Do it twice," James said in a low voice. "Second time is for me."

Luis reached for his guns.

Dex had no idea where he came from, but Joshua Bonner stepped between Dex and Luis.

"You'll have to go through me to get to my friend," Joshua said boldly.

Luis only laughed. "The marshal, he tell me all about you, boy. Fast like lightning but you can't hit a damn thing. Isn't that right?"

"No, it isn't," Joshua said. Dex was genuinely proud of him. There was no boastfulness in Joshua's voice, only simple conviction.

"Ha. It's what the marshal say to me, so don' lie."

Interesting, Dex thought, that Tom Harris would be abetting Blake and Luis. Come to think of it, Luis was supposed to be wanted for assaulting Dex in the livery stable that day. So why was the man walking around free and happy with Harris looking on.

Dex sighed. And just when he'd thought they ran into an honest man. Pity.

"I got plenty of bullets," Luis said. "I will just kill you first, Bonner. Then those two."

Joshua said nothing.

But when Luis reached for his guns, Joshua's hands flashed and his own Colts barked and bellowed. Joshua really had been putting in some practice on his accuracy.

Luis was past being able to see anything.

Luis was down like a fallen rag doll, one hole square in the middle of his forehead and three more low in his chest.

"Nice shooting, Joshua," Dex said.

Joshua grinned at him. "Thanks. I told you I was getting better."

"You did for a fact."

Tom Harris and Curtis Blake seemed more than a little surprised when they came outside—in no hurry about it though—to survey the aftermath of what they both apparently thought was to be little more than an execution.

Neither man seemed prepared to find that it was Luis on the ground and not Dexter.

Harris went pale, but Dex ignored him. The hell with Tom Harris. Dex had no interest in the man and certainly did not intend trying to rectify every wrong in the neighborhood. Winter Grove was welcome to the SOB.

And Blake was not the sort who would risk his own neck. That was what underlings were for, after all.

He looked pissed off, but he neither said nor did anything.

Dex smiled quietly to himself. If Blake was pissed off now, it would be nothing compared with what was going to happen when that team of scientists arrived.

It seemed a pity that Dex and James would be so far away when Blake discovered that he'd been had and that the Winter Grove Pixie was a fraud.

But what the hell, a man can't have everything.

"Let's gather up our stuff and get out of here," Dex said. "Personally I've had about enough of this place."

"Right behind you, white boy. Right damn behind you."

The New Action Western Series
From the creators of LONGARM!
DIAMONDBACK

Smooth as a snake—and twice as slippery—Dex Yancey is the con man's con man. Whether the game is cards, dice or gambling with your life, Dex is ready to play against the odds—and win. Ladies love him. Gamblers hate him. But *nobody* pulls one over on Dex...

☐ **DIAMONDBACK** 0-515-12568-7/$5.99

Dex didn't much cotton to the family business—a cotton plantation—but he was still mighty riled when his brother, Lewis, cheated him out of his inheritance. So Dex decided it was time to show Lewis a thing or two about brotherly love...

☐ **DIAMONDBACK #2: Texas Two-Timing**
0-515-12685-3/$5.99

While passing through Benson, Texas, Dex sees a chance to make some easy money. The local gentry challenge him to a horserace, and Dex—with a little ingenuity— comes in first place, naturally. But when he tries to collect his winnings, he's accused of cheating...

☐ **DIAMONDBACK #3: Raking in Revenge**
0-515-12753-1/$5.99

When Dex and his friend James rode into Texas they weren't looking for trouble. But they found it in a band of cross-burning hoods who leave James for dead...

☐ **DIAMONDBACK #4: Game of Chance**
0-515-12806-6/$5.99

Dex would do anything for three thousand dollars—even pose as a hitman. But pulling the trigger is another story—especially when the victim is a rich beauty.

Prices slightly higher in Canada

Payable by Visa, MC or AMEX only ($10.00 min.), No cash, checks or COD. Shipping & handling: US/Can. $2.75 for one book, $1.00 for each add'l book; Int'l $5.00 for one book, $1.00 for each add'l. Call (800) 788-6262 or (201) 933-9292, fax (201) 896-8569 or mail your orders to:

Penguin Putnam Inc. P.O. Box 12289, Dept. B Newark, NJ 07101-5289 Please allow 4-6 weeks for delivery. Foreign and Canadian delivery 6-8 weeks.	Bill my: ☐ Visa ☐ MasterCard ☐ Amex _____ (expires) Card# _____ Signature _____

Bill to:

Name _____

Address _____ City _____

State/ZIP _____ Daytime Phone # _____

Ship to:

Name _____ Book Total $ _____

Address _____ Applicable Sales Tax $ _____

City _____ Postage & Handling $ _____

State/ZIP _____ Total Amount Due $ _____

This offer subject to change without notice. Ad # 878 (5/00)

**Explore the exciting Old West with one
of the men who made it wild!**

_LONGARM AND THE NEVADA NYMPHS #240   0-515-12411-7/$4.99
_LONGARM AND THE COLORADO COUNTERFEITER #241
                                            0-515-12437-0/$4.99
_LONGARM GIANT #18: LONGARM AND THE DANISH DAMES
                                            0-515-12435-4/$5.50
_LONGARM AND THE RED-LIGHT LADIES #242   0-515-12450-8/$4.99
_LONGARM AND THE KANSAS JAILBIRD #243   0-515-12468-0/$4.99
_LONGARM #244: LONGARM AND THE DEVIL'S SISTER
                                            0-515-12485-0/$4.99
_LONGARM #245: LONGARM AND THE VANISHING VIRGIN
                                            0-515-12511-3/$4.99
_LONGARM AND THE CURSED CORPSE #246   0-515-12519-9/$4.99
_LONGARM AND THE LADY FROM TOMBSTONE #247
                                            0-515-12533-4/$4.99
_LONGARM AND THE WRONGED WOMAN #248   0-515-12556-3/$4.99
_LONGARM AND THE SHEEP WAR #249   0-515-12572-5/$4.99
_LONGARM AND THE CHAIN GANG WOMEN #250   0-515-12614-4/$4.99
_LONGARM AND THE DIARY OF MADAME VELVET #251
                                            0-515-12660-8/$4.99
_LONGARM AND THE FOUR CORNERS GANG #249   0-515-12687-X/$4.99
_LONGARM IN THE VALLEY OF SIN #253   0-515-12707-8/$4.99
_LONGARM AND THE REDHEAD'S RANSOM #254   0-515-12734-5/$4.99
_LONGARM AND THE MUSTANG MAIDEN #255   0-515-12755-8/$4.99
_LONGARM AND THE DYNAMITE DAMSEL #256   0-515-12770-1/$4.99
_LONGARM AND THE NEVADA BELLYDANCER #257   0-515-12790-6/$4.99
_LONGARM #258: LONGARM AND THE PISTOLERO
                 PRINCESS   0-515-12808-2/$4.99

Prices slightly higher in Canada

Payable by Visa, MC or AMEX only ($10.00 min.), No cash, checks or COD. Shipping & handling:
US/Can. $2.75 for one book, $1.00 for each add'l book; Int'l $5.00 for one book, $1.00 for each
add'l. Call (800) 788-6262 or (201) 933-9292, fax (201) 896-8569 or mail your orders to:

Penguin Putnam Inc.   Bill my: ❑ Visa ❑ MasterCard ❑ Amex _____ (expires)
P.O. Box 12289, Dept. B
Newark, NJ 07101-5289   Card# _____
Please allow 4-6 weeks for delivery.   Signature _____
Foreign and Canadian delivery 6-8 weeks.

Bill to:
Name _____
Address _____ City _____
State/ZIP _____ Daytime Phone # _____
Ship to:
Name _____ Book Total $ _____
Address _____ Applicable Sales Tax $ _____
City _____ Postage & Handling $ _____
State/ZIP _____ Total Amount Due $ _____

This offer subject to change without notice.   Ad # 201 (3/00)

JAKE LOGAN
TODAY'S HOTTEST ACTION WESTERN!

☐ SLOCUM AND THE WOLF HUNT #237	0-515-12413-3/$4.99
☐ SLOCUM AND THE BARONESS #238	0-515-12436-2/$4.99
☐ SLOCUM AND THE COMANCHE PRINCESS #239	0-515-12449-4/$4.99
☐ SLOCUM AND THE LIVE OAK BOYS #240	0-515-12467-2/$4.99
☐ SLOCUM#241: SLOCUM AND THE BIG THREE	0-515-12484-2/$4.99
☐ SLOCUM #242: SLOCUM AT SCORPION BEND	0-515-12510-5/$4.99
☐ SLOCUM AND THE BUFFALO HUNTER #243	0-515-12518-0/$4.99
☐ SLOCUM AND THE YELLOW ROSE OF TEXAS #244	0-515-12532-6/$4.99
☐ SLOCUM AND THE LADY FROM ABILINE #245	0-515-12555-5/$4.99
☐ SLOCUM GIANT: SLOCUM AND THE THREE WIVES	0-515-12569-5/$5.99
☐ SLOCUM AND THE CATTLE KING #246	0-515-12571-7/$4.99
☐ SLOCUM #247: DEAD MAN'S SPURS	0-515-12613-6/$4.99
☐ SLOCUM #248: SHOWDOWN AT SHILOH	0-515-12659-4/$4.99
☐ SLOCUM AND THE KETCHEM GANG #249	0-515-12686-1/$4.99
☐ SLOCUM AND THE JERSEY LILY #250	0-515-12706-X/$4.99
☐ SLOCUM AND THE GAMBLER'S WOMAN #251	0-515-12733-7/$4.99
☐ SLOCUM AND THE GUNRUNNERS #252	0-515-12754-X/$4.99
☐ SLOCUM AND THE NEBRASKA STORM #253	0-515-12769-8/$4.99
☐ SLOCUM #254: SLOCUM'S CLOSE CALL	0-515-12789-2/$4.99
☐ SLOCUM AND THE UNDERTAKER #255	0-515-12807-4/$4.99
☐ SLOCUM AND THE POMO CHIEF #256	0-515-12838-4/$4.99

Prices slightly higher in Canada

Payable by Visa, MC or AMEX only ($10.00 min.), No cash, checks or COD. Shipping & handling:
US/Can. $2.75 for one book, $1.00 for each add'l book; Int'l $5.00 for one book, $1.00 for each
add'l. Call (800) 788-6262 or (201) 933-9292, fax (201) 896-8569 or mail your orders to:
#(12/99)

Penguin Putnam Inc. P.O. Box 12289, Dept. B Newark, NJ 07101-5289 Please allow 4-6 weeks for delivery. Foreign and Canadian delivery 6-8 weeks.	Bill my: ☐ Visa ☐ MasterCard ☐ Amex _____ (expires) Card# _____ Signature _____

Bill to:

Name _____

Address _____ City _____

State/ZIP _____ Daytime Phone # _____

Ship to:

Name _____ Book Total $ _____

Address _____ Applicable Sales Tax $ _____

City _____ Postage & Handling $ _____

State/ZIP _____ Total Amount Due $ _____

This offer subject to change without notice.   Ad # 202 (4/00)